MURDER ABOARD THE FLYING SCOTSMAN

A GINGER GOLD MYSTERY #8

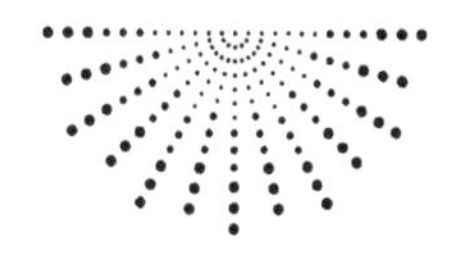

LEE STRAUSS

Murder Aboard the Flying Scotsman

Cover by Steven Novak

Illustrations by Tasia Strauss

La Plume Press

3205-415 Commonwealth Road

Kelowna, BC, Canada

V4V 2M4

www.laplumepress.com

ISBN: 9781774090077

PRAISE FOR GINGER GOLD

"Clever and entertaining, you'll love this charming Golden Age mystery series. And the fashion is to die for!" **- Molly C. Quinn, actress, *Castle***

"Another deftly crafted mystery by the master of the genre..." Midwest Book Review

"I rank Lee Strauss as the best living cozy mystery writer. Her characters are believable but interesting, her stories are fun to follow and her use of language is superb. She makes the 1920s come alive in my imagination. **I constantly read cozies and Lee's Lady Gold Mysteries are the very best."** - LoriLynn, Amazon reviewer

GINGER GOLD MYSTERIES

(IN ORDER)

Murder on the SS *Rosa*
Murder at Hartigan House
Murder at Bray Manor
Murder at Feathers & Flair
Murder at the Mortuary
Murder at Kensington Gardens
Murder at St. George's Church
Murder Aboard the Flying Scotsman
Murder at the Boat Club
Murder on Eaton Square
Murder by Plum Pudding
Murder on Fleet Street

CHAPTER ONE

"I feel like a gooseberry," Felicia Gold whimpered. "How daft of me to join you on your wedding journey."

"You and many others," Ginger returned with a smile.

Seated aboard the Flying Scotsman, England's fastest train, opposite her former sister-in-law, Felicia shifted her weight and crossed her legs. "I *could* move to another compartment. Or even another carriage. I don't mind second class."

"Don't be silly," Ginger said. She turned to the handsome gentleman who sat as close as he could. "Basil and I love having you, don't we, darling?"

Basil Reed's hazel eyes twinkled as he gazed into his new bride's beaming face. "Of course."

"Your gushing happiness is starting to make me feel

sickly," Felicia said. "At least you'll only have to put up with me half of the way."

Ginger stroked the small Boston terrier curled on her lap. Boss, short for Boston, had been a gift from her father after the Great War. She'd returned to their Beacon Hill home from France without her late husband, Lord Daniel Gold, who had perished in battle. Boss snored softly and was quite unperturbed by the foreign surroundings on board the train.

Smiling at Felicia, Ginger asked, "Is Miss Dansby meeting you at York station?"

"Yes," Felicia answered. "And her fiancé, Mr. George Pierce. I'm very curious to meet him. Irene describes him in her letters like he's a god. Not a physical blemish or character flaw to be found."

Ginger laughed. "Must be love!" She patted Basil's arm.

Basil raised Ginger's hand and kissed it. "*You* are perfection itself, Mrs. Reed."

"Please stop!" Felicia moaned. "Or I just might have to throw myself out the window."

"If you must, please do so before the train starts moving," Basil said wryly.

Through the glass compartment door, Ginger caught sight of an elderly lady dressed in black apparel. Assisted by a stick-thin porter, she entered the carriage. She appeared trapped in the nineteenth century with her tight-fitting coat, her long, heavy skirt, and a boat of a hat pinned to white hair that was piled into a bun on the top of her head. Her face was concealed by a thick black veil.

Despite using a cane to assist her slow, stilted gait, the lady stood upright and was most obviously wearing a corset. Ginger had a fleeting thought of Ambrosia, Daniel's grandmother and Ginger's house companion. Had she not had the influence of the younger set in her life, Ambrosia would undoubtedly have continued to resemble this latest passenger. Unfortunately, Ambrosia's new liberties didn't make her any happier, and the perpetual scowl and overall distrust of "this wayward generation" remained.

The lady nodded at the empty upholstered seat beside Felicia and said in a rather husky voice to the lad assisting her, "This is far enough."

When the porter opened the door, she said to Felicia, "You don't mind, do you? I'd rather not walk more than necessary, and my seat is in the last compartment down the corridor."

Basil answered for them all. "You're welcome to join us."

The porter assisted the lady into the plush seat. "Such lovely polished teak and brass! And these velvet chairs are simply marvellous," she said. "Thank goodness someone had the brains to make the backs high enough to support one's neck. I'll warn you good people in advance; I might embarrass myself by falling asleep. At my age, one tends to nod off without intending to."

The whistle blew, and the green carriages of the Flying Scotsman slowly and laboriously inched forwards. Loud rhythmic clanking came from the steel wheels. Gears screeched in response. With each rotation, motion increased in speed. White plumes of steam gushed past the windows and blocked their view of King's Cross Station.

"I'm needed in Edinburgh, for a funeral," their new companion offered.

"I'm sorry," Ginger said. "Is it someone close?"

"No. I barely knew him. I just like going to funerals. I know it sounds morbid, but I do have a fascination with death. It's my age, you see."

Ginger shared a stunned look with Felicia. The lady was quite forthright and clearly dressed as one in mourning.

"I was at the hanging of Susan Newell, a year ago today," the elderly lady continued. "What a spectacle that was! The first woman to hang in Scotland in fifty years. She refused the white hood. Her eyes nearly . . ." She opened her gloved hand by her eye and mimicked an explosion. "It wasn't pretty, let me tell you."

Oh, mercy. Ginger had to bite her lip to keep from

laughing. "A funeral should prove to be rather boring after that."

"Oh no. It's a double funeral. The man was *murdered.* By his wife. Then she took her own life. A big family scandal with a bundle of money involved. When I read about it in the paper, I knew I had to go."

Felicia's eyes widened with incredulity.

"Do forgive my rudeness," the lady said. "I'm Mrs. Simms."

"I'm L—" Ginger stopped herself in time. She'd almost introduced herself as Lady Gold, a title she'd given up when she'd married Basil. "I'm Mrs. Reed. This is my husband Chief Inspector Reed, and my sister-in-law, Miss Gold."

Mrs. Simms turned her head sharply towards Basil.

"Are the two of you acquainted?" Ginger asked looking between them.

"No, no. I do apologise for staring," Mrs. Simms replied, tilting her veiled head towards Ginger. "Sometimes my mind goes blank, goes on a bit of a holiday. The lament of old age." Frowning at Basil she added, "A police officer you say?"

"Yes, madam."

"What takes you to Edinburgh, Chief Inspector? A case for Scotland Yard, I presume?"

Basil patted Ginger's gloved hand. "My wife and I are on our honeymoon."

"Oh, how marvellous. Congratulations," Mrs. Simms said, beaming. "I'm sure you'll have a lovely time. The highlands are splendid in the autumn season."

"I was there as a child," Ginger said, "but it's exciting to take the Flying Scotsman."

"Shaves off two hours," Mrs. Simms offered. "Such a difference, especially at my age. And I love travelling on something so new." She inhaled deeply. "Still smells like fresh paint and new fabric. It's yet to be blighted with bad experiences like death and derailment. Or a robbery. You might be too young to remember, but the world's first train robbery happened in England."

"You're referring to the Great Gold Robbery of 1855," Basil said.

"Yes, indeed. It was quite a sensation. I was a youngster at the time and impressionable. My village talked about little else for months."

Mrs. Simms didn't, as Ginger was beginning to fear, talk their ears off and had, in fact, fallen asleep as she'd predicted. Felicia lost herself in a mystery novel. Boss, a terrific sleeper as well, jerked on occasion. *The result of some adventurous dream*, Ginger thought with a grin. She was content to lean into Basil and watch the scenery.

Presently, the conductor stepped into the carriage and announced loudly, "First sitting for lunch."

Felicia put her book down. “I’d like to dine. I’m feeling rather peckish.”

Ginger took a moment to examine her reflection in the window, patted her red bob, and reinforced the curled tips that rested below high cheekbones.

Mrs. Simms’ head bobbed up. Ginger could barely make out her eyes behind the black veil except to notice that they had opened.

“What’s happening?” Mrs. Simms’ voice was pitched so low that Ginger thought to offer her a glass of water.

“It’s first sitting for lunch,” Ginger explained. “Would you care to join us?”

“I was having the most interesting dream. A dismembered body was floating alongside the train.” She turned towards the window as if she expected to see such a gruesome sight and then ducked her chin. “If you don’t mind, I think I’d rather fall back to sleep.”

In the dining car, Felicia confessed, “This will sound snooty, but I’m glad Mrs. Simms didn’t join us. I dare say, her mind is frightfully *alarming*.”

CHAPTER TWO

The dining carriage was located to the rear of first class, and for the most part, was for the benefit of the first-class customers. Second- and third-class passengers tended to bring a packed lunch.

The menu was slight but what was offered was tempting. Ginger ordered grilled salmon on toast with fruit juice and coffee whilst Basil and Felicia chose beef and mushroom pie along with pots of tea.

The pastoral view beyond the window breezed by at an impressive speed. Flocks of sheep dotted drying pastures, cattle roamed with large bells hanging from thick necks, and horses pulled farm equipment readying fields for winter.

The tea and coffee were served immediately, and Ginger removed her elbow-length, white satin gloves and placed them neatly to the side.

Felicia did the same. "How fast do you think we are going?" she asked.

"Close to a hundred miles an hour," Ginger answered. "There's an outstanding exhibit about the Flying Scotsman at the British Empire Exhibition."

"That's frightfully fast," Felicia said. She adjusted her felt cloche hat as if the wind outside had caused the floral display pinned over her right ear to shift out of place.

Ginger pointed to a structure along the rails as they approached one of the many villages on route. A ladder was attached to a small platform about six feet tall. On it were a couple of posts with foreign items hanging from them. "What is that?"

"That's for picking up and dropping off the post," Basil said. "See the leather bags attached to that wooden platform and pole apparatus? The mail is secured inside. In seconds, bags left hanging from the postage carriage are dispatched into that wide netting you see on this side of the platform. Moments later, the train scoops up the bags hanging on the apparatus, which land in the post office van."

"How efficient," Ginger said as she watched the exchange.

Basil agreed. "Surprisingly so."

"Good old Royal Mail!" Felicia said.

Their food arrived, and Ginger covered her lap

with a cotton napkin. She didn't want to risk staining her Paul Poiret silk frock. She was quite aware that the emerald green with the gold embroidered design emphasised the green of her eyes and the gold highlights in her red hair. Basil had declared the dress a favourite of his, and Ginger thought it fitting to wear on the first day of their wedding journey.

An attractive couple entered the dining car. She, blonde and stylish with a salon-created Marcelled bob, wore a lovely day frock. A noticeable yet lovely mole rested on the corner of her lips. He was dressed in a pinstripe, well-pressed suit and what appeared to be Italian leather shoes. The lady hung possessively to the gentleman's arm, but her eyes didn't bespeak of romantic love, instead, they seemed serious and nervous.

"Irene?" Felicia said.

Shock crossed the lady's face before morphing into a bright, inviting smile. "Felicia! Darling!" She took the few steps down the narrow aisle and Felicia shifted out of the booth. They embraced and shared kisses on the cheeks.

"What are you doing on this train?" Felicia said. "You're meant to greet me in York when I arrive."

"Was that today?" Irene said, mascara-laden lashes blinking. "I thought you were arriving next week."

"Oh my hat!" Felicia said. "Did I make an error?

I'll have to check my diary, but I was certain it was today. I feel foolish."

"No, you mustn't. It's probably my mistake. You know how scatterbrained I can be. Oh, Felicia, let me introduce my fiancé, Mr. George Pierce."

Felicia stretched out her hand and shook Mr. Pierce's amiably. Mr. Pierce smiled. "It's a pleasure to meet you."

To Ginger and Basil, Felicia added, "And this is my good friend Miss Irene Dansby. Irene, this is my sister-in—"

Taking pity on Felicia, Ginger stepped in. "I'm Mrs. Reed, and this is my husband, Mr. Reed." Now that Ginger had remarried, it was an adjustment for all to get used to her new name and family status.

Mr. Pierce said, "How do you do?"

Felicia took aim at her friend. "You were in London, and you didn't bother to visit?"

"This was a quick trip to see the Opera," Irene explained. "One night only. Otherwise, you know I would've rung you."

"I'm surprised we didn't run into one another at Kings Cross," Ginger said.

Irene glanced at Mr. Pierce then answered, "It is a rather busy place."

Basil contributed to the conversation with a nod. "Indeed."

"I'm so glad to finally meet Felicia's friend from York," Ginger said. "She speaks of you often. Warmly, of course. You must join us."

Felicia jumped in. "Unless you'd rather be alone?"

"There's a pressing issue we need to discuss," George Pierce said. "We'll catch up with you in York . . . if that's okay."

Felicia's face dropped, but she recovered quickly. "Certainly."

"My diary is packed in my luggage," Felicia said once she, Ginger and Basil were settled in at their table. "As soon as I get settled in York, I'm going to check. I just can't believe I made an error as grave as this."

"It's not so grave an error," Ginger said. "It happens. Besides, my bet is on Miss Dansby. She did say she was a scatterbrain. How did you and Miss Dansby become acquainted?"

"We're childhood friends," Felicia said, no longer able to rein in her annoyance. "We attended the same school in Chesterton." Her gaze shot to the table where Miss Dansby and Mr. Pierce drank coffee then focused on something out of the window. "Are we slowing down? Are we at York already?"

The loud screeching of the large metal wheels could be heard inside the dining car as the train came to an abrupt stop. Plates shifted along the tabletops and stopped at the lip around the edge. Diners were knocked about, some nearly losing their seats.

"What's happening?" Felicia yelped.

The door to the dining car opened from the first-class side of the carriage, and a man dressed in a railway guard's uniform entered. His eyes scanned the room, and when they found Basil, he headed straight to their table.

"Chief Inspector Reed?"

"Yes."

"I'm sorry to disturb you, but we saw your name on the passenger manifest, and well, there's been a . . . uh . . . disturbance. Mr. Tippet, the engineer, has requested your assistance.

CHAPTER THREE

My honeymoon is beginning to resemble my wedding day, the words snapped in Basil's mind. Circumstances beyond his control were commandeering his plans for the day. All he wanted was to be alone with his bride. To hold hands, be alone amongst strangers, and to forget about work.

He had, as the Americans loved to say, struck out. Felicia travelling the same day on the same train was pure bad luck. He couldn't very well have asked her to sit elsewhere, could he? The last thing he needed was to make the household of women he'd only just moved in with have a reason to hold ill feelings against him. And, it seemed, Felicia had made a mistake with the date after all!

And now, this "disturbance," whatever it was. The

diminutive railwayman looked distinctly distressed. Pale, with a slight tremble.

Basil stood. "Your name, sir?"

"Burgess. I'm head guard on this route. Please follow me."

As Basil knew she would, Ginger stepped in behind him.

"Oh, I don't think a lady should join us, sir."

"It's quite all right." He grinned at Ginger. As always, she was dazzlingly beautiful. "My wife isn't like ordinary ladies."

Burgess stood on his toes to whisper in Basil's ear. "All the same, sir. There's been a death."

Basil reassured him. "She'll be fine."

Ginger smiled in a way that made Basil long for her. If only this blasted train ride would end.

"Felicia," she said. "Do go and see that Mrs. Simms is all right."

Felicia wrinkled her nose in displeasure. "What about you?"

"I'm going with Basil. As soon as I find out what's happened, I'll let you know."

Felicia sighed. "Very well. I suppose I should collect my things anyway."

Basil waited for Ginger to step in front of him then gently guided her by the small of her back. He loved that he could touch her in these little, intimate ways. If only they could get off this stifling train! Shuffling along the narrow corridor behind the wiry Burgess made him feel large and bulky. He didn't mind short routes or even being underground on the tube system in London, but hours-long travel in a can of sardines made him feel short of breath.

Burgess paused outside the door of the next carriage. "This is where the post is sorted and delivered."

"Chief Inspector Reed was just explaining how the post travelled by train through the country," Ginger said. "Quite fascinating."

"Yes, well." Mr. Burgess' eyes locked onto Basil's. "It's rather gruesome, sir." He nodded towards Ginger. "Are you quite sure?

Ginger glanced at Basil with a look of amusement. Or was that irritation? She could hide her emotions when she wanted to. A skill, among many others, his new wife had learned whilst working for the British Secret Service during the Great War.

His wife didn't like to talk about her time there, or perhaps, she was forbidden to, but Basil did know that Ginger had seen many gruesome sights involving dead bodies. Not only in France but on the streets of London. She'd proved to be a rather good amateur sleuth in the short time Basil had known her, and had assisted him in quite a few tricky cases.

Burgess knocked on the door, and it was opened by a bespectacled man with thinning hair. His trousers were held up by leather braces over a crumpled white shirt.

"This is Mr. Doring," Burgess said. "He's head of operations for the mail coach on this train."

"Hello, Mr. Doring," Basil said, shaking the man's hand.

It was damp with nerves, and Doring quickly shoved it back into his pockets.

"I'm Chief Inspector Reed, and this is my wife, Mrs. Reed. I understand there's been a death."

"Yes. A very shocking and unfortunate situation."

"Do you suspect foul play? Perhaps the victim—a man is it?" After a nod in the affirmative, Basil continued, "Perhaps he suffered a heart attack. I understand there's a lot of pressure to perform one's duties quickly and accurately. Is it possible he couldn't manage the stress?"

Burgess and Doring exchanged glances. "He's not one of ours," Doring said.

"Oh? Did the fellow lose his way?" Basil asked, pulling at his collar. He couldn't blame the bloke for leaving in search of some air.

"No, sir," Doring said. "He came in from outside."

"Outside?" Ginger said. "Was he a stowaway?"

"No, madam."

Basil had had enough of the riddles. "Show us the body, please."

Another look passed between the men. "It's right there, on the floor."

Basil frowned. There was no man lying on the floor, dead or alive. He glared at the men. "It's a criminal offence to waste the time of the police."

Ginger touched his elbow. "Basil. It looks like blood is coming from that mailbag."

The leather pouch had been opened, but it lay in a manner where the opening faced the other way. Basil squatted and peered inside. "Blimey!"

CHAPTER FOUR

Despite protestations from Mr. Burgess, Ginger bent low to view the contents.

Oh, mercy!

Inside the letter bag, a gruesome, washed-out face with lifeless eyes stared back at her.

"A decapitation."

A middle-aged man in a guard's uniform entered the carriage. His eyes locked on the letter bag on the wooden floor. "So, it's true, eh?" He removed his cap and palmed his short-cropped oiled hair before returning it. "I was hopin' it was a bad joke and was ready to sack someone for causin' an unnecessary delay. The Flying Scotsman has a reputation for speed and timeliness."

"I'm London CID," Basil said. "This is Yorkshire jurisdiction."

Mr. Tippet's dark eyes were beseeching. "If you'd be so kind as to step in until the police arrive. I've sent an electric telegraph."

"Very well." Basil turned to all the men in the space. "No one is to leave this carriage until I say." Out of habit, Basil searched his pockets but came up empty. "Would any of you gentlemen have a notepad and pencil?"

With all the paper in the post office van, Ginger expected it was quite likely and was proven correct. Mr. Doring scrambled to gather the objects and handed them to Basil. The poor fellow trembled terribly.

"Thank you, my good man. Now, if you will, please relay the sequence of events that led to this unfortunate situation."

Mr. Doring held thin arms against his chest. "Well, it's such a shock, I'm not sure where to begin. It was just a normal workday. I started my shift in London and came directly to the post office van as did all the gentlemen present."

"I'll need names after we're finished here," Basil said. "Continue on."

"The men were doing their usual business, sorting letters and the like. The letter bags ready to be dispatched were hung in the leather drop bags on the hooks just outside that door."

The post office van had a sliding exterior door, now closed.

"Our bags are dropped, and the ones hanging on the exchange apparatus are delivered."

"Where do they land?" Ginger asked.

Mr. Doring pointed to the floor of the carriage. "Right here. They land with a bang, and we close the door. It's quite a racket with the whistle going throughout the operation.

"And this is the pouch that was picked up?" Basil said.

"One of two." He pointed to one that was opened with letters exposed.

"What town did it come from, precisely?" Ginger asked.

"Doncaster. It's the last drop before York."

Basil scribbled notes. "Does anyone here recognise the face?"

Mr. Doring hesitated before answering. "Well, it's hard to tell for sure, with all the blood and bloating, but it does look a bit like Oscar Wright."

"Textile tycoon?" Basil's voice betrayed a slight note of shock. The uninitiated would likely not have noticed, but Ginger knew her husband well.

"Are you acquainted?" Ginger asked.

"Just nominally. He attended a party in London where I was a guest."

Ginger turned back to the supervisor. "Has a telegraph been sent to the police surgeon? In case this isn't Mr. Wright's head. We wouldn't want to start a nasty rumour."

"Yes, madam," Mr. Tippet said. "I requested a doctor as well."

"Has anything been touched or moved?" Basil asked.

"I dragged the pouch away from the open door so we could close it," Mr. Doring said. "Straightaway I could tell something wasn't right. The shape and weight of it. I opened the straps, and when I saw what was inside, I fell on my ars—excuse me, madam, fell on my backside and scrambled away. It was a real shock, I'll tell you."

"It hasn't been moved or touched since then?" Basil asked.

"No, sir."

Basil addressed the guard. "Mr. Burgess, is there a place these men could wait away from this unpleasantness? I'm sure they'd like to sit down."

"I'll find a spot, sir."

"They're not to mix with anyone else until they've given their statements. We'll need to take fingerprints before we can release them."

A porter knocked and poked his head inside. Ginger noted how Basil stepped in front of the mailbag to conceal it. Once the porter's gaze located the engineer he announced, "The police have arrived, sir."

"Show them in," Mr. Tippet said.

Shortly afterwards, a barrel-chested man joined Ginger, Basil, Mr. Doring, and Mr. Tippet. Ginger assumed he was the lead inspector and his two young uniformed companions were constables. A slender man, around Ginger's age of thirty, set a black medical kit on the floor.

"I'm Inspector Sullivan," the large man said, his words were low and gravelly.

Quite likely due to a cigarette habit, Ginger thought as she noted the nicotine-stained fingers of his right hand. He appeared to be out of breath.

He motioned to the slimmer man. "This is Dr. Chapman, York's police surgeon."

Basil responded to the introductions. "I'm Chief Inspector Reed of Scotland Yard. My wife and I are passengers. Mr. Tippet saw my name on the passenger list and asked if I would assist until you arrived."

"Thank you. If you wouldn't mind bringing me up to speed, it would be much appreciated."

"Of course."

Inspector Sullivan's gaze darted briefly to Ginger. "Your wife is welcome to go back to her seat."

"She'd prefer to stay if you don't mind."

Looking very much as if he did mind, the York

inspector frowned. "All right, then. What do you know?"

"The head was in the mail pouch dropped from Doncaster," Basil replied. "Mr. Doring, the supervisor, was the first and only to see the face. He says it resembles Oscar Wright."

"Mr. Wright?" The police surgeon said. The doctor was young and intense in appearance with dark, oiled hair combed sharply to one side.

"Do you know the man?" Basil asked.

Inspector Sullivan answered for all of them. "Everyone who lives in York knows him."

Dr. Chapman mimicked what Ginger and Basil had done before him: squatted, looked into the bag, and grimaced. "Looks like Wright to me." He shone a light into the victim's eyes. "Vitreous humour is glazed over."

"What does that mean?" Inspector Sullivan said impatiently.

"The vitreous humour is the clear gel between the lens and the retina of the eye. It's gone opaque, which means the man's been dead about eight hours."

Ginger checked her wristwatch. Twenty-five minutes past two. "He was killed around dawn."

"Let me have a look." The inspector grunted as he knelt. "I recognise the scar above the left eyebrow.

Took a right hook from a disgruntled employee about a decade ago. That's him all right."

"I'll take the head, along with the bag, to the lab," Dr. Chapman said. "Maybe the killer left something behind."

"What about the Flying Scotsman," the engineer asked. "We mustn't hold up the tracks."

"Can we uncouple some of the carriages?"

"There's a siding about a mile north. Which carriages, sir?"

Inspector Sullivan cast a glance at Basil before replying. "If I'm to understand correctly, only persons in the first class and the first-class dining carriages could've accessed the post office van."

"That's correct, sir," Mr. Tippet said.

"Also, the luggage van," Inspector Sullivan added.

"The luggage van, sir?" Mr. Tippet said.

Basil nodded. "In case the rest of the body has been packed away in another manner."

CHAPTER FIVE

When on the move, the Flying Scotsman gave one the sensation of flight—like a low-flying swan—hooting, singing, chugging along past fields of grazing cattle, and through low valleys. There was no quicker way to travel, other than aeroplane, which wasn't a form of travel easily accessible to the British, no matter their social standing. Although now, with the new Imperial Airways, continental trips were feasible for those with a steady stomach and a steadier bank account.

Usually, train passengers were amiable, polite, and whether the loquacious sort or quiet, travel along the rails gave one a feeling of anticipation and, even though one sat and waited out the time, a sense of accomplishment.

A carriage at a standstill was another matter altogether. Now the atmosphere was charged with frustration, discomfort, and hostility.

The man and woman from two compartments back stood anxiously in the corridor, he with a cigarette dangling from chapped lips. They appeared to be in their late forties; she had soft full cheeks and an ample bosom, and he, a long face with sharp features and short limbs.

"Why have we stopped? This is most certainly not York." The woman's voice carried along the carriage.

"The steward said there's a problem with the post office van," the man replied. "At least we're moving again, albeit at a snail's pace."

Ginger whispered to Basil, "I overheard the porter calling them by the name of Fisher."

The carriage jerked causing Mrs. Fisher to shriek. "Sydney, what's happening?"

Basil answered for the beleaguered husband. "Unfortunately, this carriage along with a few others is being uncoupled from the rest of the train."

Two businessmen had joined them, the taller one also lighting up. "Did I hear you say we're being sidelined?" He released blue smoke into the air.

Ginger would've opened a corridor window had it not been so cold out.

The man continued to protest. "We're first class! If anyone should continue, it should be us."

His companion commiserated. "I certainly agree. As soon as we reach Edinburgh, I'm writing a letter of complaint.

Basil whispered in Ginger's ear. "I'm going to check about something. I'll be back shortly."

The aggravation growing from the small crowd was palpable, and Ginger felt she should perhaps explain. "The matter in the post office van is complicated. There is a good reason that these particular carriages must be delayed."

The businessmen stared at Ginger with derision. The shorter one spoke first. "Forgive me, madam, but who, might I ask, are you?"

"I'm Mrs. Reed." She glanced over her shoulder in the direction that Basil had disappeared. "My husband is Chief Inspector Reed of Scotland Yard. He's assisting in the investigation."

The taller man replied. "I'm Mr. Claude Murray, and this is my business partner, Mr. Robert Whitley. Please forgive our agitation. It seems we're destined to miss a rather important meeting."

"There is nothing to apologise for," Ginger said graciously. "We are all being inconvenienced, I should say."

Ginger's response cooled the tempers of the disgruntled passengers, at least for the time being. It explained how a *lady* might *know* things.

An attractive lady wearing a stunning black-and-white satin frock with a modern geometric pattern entered the corridor from her compartment at the back. She motioned with a black-satin-gloved hand for Ginger to approach. "Excuse me, Mrs. Reed is it? I couldn't help but overhear."

Ginger eased along the narrow passage. "Yes?"

"I'm Lady Pennington."

Ginger recognised the lady, a well-known Scottish opera singer. She'd had the pleasure of seeing her perform once.

The singer lowered her voice. "I really do find this situation insufferable. Perhaps there is a way I could discreetly disembark?"

Ginger understood the thinking of Lady Pennington well and for a moment, a split second really, she missed her recently discarded title. It shamed Ginger to think that, like Lady Pennington, she had grown used to flaunting her title to get special treatment, and that it had, for the most part, worked. She didn't blame Lady Pennington for expecting her to jump to attention and hurry to pull strings to see that her request was approved, but she couldn't help but feel annoyed. Not only at Lady Pennington but at herself, because it was highly likely, had Ginger been in this situation as Lady Gold, that she would've attempted the same thing.

"I'm dreadfully sorry, Lady Pennington," Ginger said politely, "but I'm afraid you'll have to wait the same as the others. You see," Ginger drew closer, giving the lady a teasing morsel of inside information, "there's been a suspicious event."

Before Lady Pennington could ask questions, Ginger moved quickly to her own compartment, passing Miss Dansby and Mr. Pierce who were holding hands and staring out of the window. An older lady wearing a simple, brown tunic frock was seated across from Irene Dansby. She had a wrinkly concave face with small features and wore a short-brimmed felt hat over a brown bob. None appeared to be enjoying their travels.

Ginger arrived at her compartment and Felicia, wrapped in a fur-trimmed stole, grabbed Ginger by the hand, nearly tugging her into her seat. "Where were you? You've been gone for ages? Why has the train stopped?"

"No need to break my arm," Ginger replied.

Boss woke up and whimpered. He climbed onto Ginger's lap, and she stroked his soft fur.

"I'm sorry," Felicia said. "I'm just frustrated. First, with Irene acting so strangely, and now this?" Felicia stretched her neck to peer out of the window. "Are we being taken off the line? What on earth is happening?"

"You must calm yourself, Felicia. Perhaps I can get us some tea."

"I *have* tea."

"Oh, yes," Ginger said, noting the small tea set on the mini sideboard. "Well, there's been a death."

"Oh dear," Felicia said, suddenly calmer. "Who died?"

"The identity isn't certain, but it appears to be Oscar Wright?"

"The textile millionaire?"

Ginger blinked hard at her sister-in-law. "You knew him?"

"Not personally. He's been in all the rags. He made heaps providing uniforms in the war. Old as the hills and still swinging with the girls if you know what I mean. Or he was. He had a stroke or something recently, so sort of old news."

Ginger focused her gaze on the empty seat in front of her. "Have you seen Mrs. Simms?"

Felicia pushed loose strands of her finger waves back in place. "She wasn't here when I returned from the dining carriage."

"That's odd," Ginger said. "I made a point of checking all the compartments and passengers. Everyone is accounted for except her."

Felicia's eyes widened and sparkled. "Perhaps Mrs.

Simms was an apparition? One couldn't clearly see her face. Perhaps because she didn't *have* one."

Ginger laughed. "Oh! I do love your fanciful imagination, Felicia."

From Ginger's position in the compartment—she'd taken Basil's aisle seat, for the moment, so she could keep an eye on things—she saw that the door connecting first class to the dining car was open. One of Inspector Sullivan's constables stepped through and was now making his way down the corridor. He stopped at each compartment to make an announcement.

When he reached Ginger and Felicia, he nodded in recognition at Ginger then said. "I'm PC Mulgrew." On seeing Boss, his face softened. "Hello, puppy."

"This is Boss," Ginger said. Boss' stubby tail started wagging as if Ginger had flipped a switch. "You can stroke him," she said. "He's very friendly."

"Thank you, madam, but I'm on duty. I'm informing the passengers about the news you are already privy to."

"I'm sure it's quite a shocking tale," Ginger said. "How are they taking it?"

"The first question is always 'Who?' which I can't answer at this time, and the second question is 'When can we get on with our journey?' which I also can't answer."

"An unsatisfactory conversation for both parties," Ginger said with a smile.

One side of the young constable's mouth pulled up. "Indeed."

"By the way, Constable Mulgrew, have you seen an elderly widow, dressed in black and a veiled hat, on board anywhere?"

The constable shook his head then adjusted the strap of his helmet. "I'll keep an eye out for her, madam."

"Do you want me to go and look for her?" Felicia asked.

Ginger noticed the book, *The Man in the Brown Suit*, resting open on Felicia's lap and grinned. "Thank you for offering, but I'll go. I want to see what Basil is up to anyway. You'll keep an eye on Boss?"

"Of course."

"Stay with Felicia, Boss," Ginger instructed as she set him down on Mrs. Simms' empty seat. "I shouldn't be too long."

Ginger nearly bumped into Basil in the corridor. He grabbed her by the waist and pulled her close.

"Basil!" Ginger felt herself blush. They were alone in the corridor, but Felicia could still see them through the glass. Thankfully, she'd been too engrossed in her novel to notice.

"I couldn't resist," Basil said drawing away. He

tugged on the ends of his waistcoat. "I promise to keep my hands to myself until we get off this blasted train."

"And when will that be?"

"Well, it seems Sullivan's chief constable has requested I continue to help with the investigation since I'm on board anyway."

"I get the feeling Inspector Sullivan's not the type of officer to be pleased with outside help."

"You're right on that count. His face was as red as a beetroot when he made the offer."

"What did you say?"

He grinned. "I told him I had to ask my wife."

Ginger patted his arm. "Oh, you did not."

"No, I didn't say that. But it is supposed to be our wedding journey, and it would mean our first night will be spent in York."

"I'm assuming that will be the case, regardless."

"So, I have your approval?" Basil asked.

"Of course. Though don't expect me to be sitting on my hands whilst I'm waiting."

Basil reached for her again, but she stepped back with a look of mischief. "You promised, Mr. Reed. Now, don't you have a case to solve?"

CHAPTER SIX

Basil and Sullivan had cleared the dining car to conduct interviews. The fingerprinting had been done and the crime scene marked off and sealed. Each letter-sorting man was brought in alone and given a seat opposite the officers. Their names, addresses, work schedules, and job duties were recorded. Also noted was whether they'd done any business with Wright. To a man, the answer to that question was 'no.'

The second to last of the group was Doring, the post office van manager.

"Mr. Doring," Sullivan began. "Please state your full name and address."

"Morris Doring. 321 Royal Way, East London."

"Would you mind walking through your steps today," Basil said.

"I left for work at five o'clock and took the underground. Entered the post office van at six. I'm the manager, so my main duty is to make sure systems run smoothly and that the men stay at pace. It's my head if we miss a drop-off."

Basil narrowed his eyes at the unfortunate pun. Doring didn't seem to notice.

"Did you ever have the opportunity to meet Mr. Oscar Wright?"

"No, sir. Never had the pleasure."

"When does your shift end?" Sullivan asked.

"Once we reach Edinburgh. Spend the night, then make the trip back."

"You may go, Mr. Doring," Basil said. "We'll find you if we have any more questions."

"He's a bit of a weasel, isn't he?" Sullivan said under his breath. "Something about him just doesn't sit right."

"How so?" Basil asked, feeling the same thing.

"I don't know. Just a hunch."

Their final interview was with Burgess, railway security. After the opening questions, Basil asked him to relay his footsteps for the day.

"Well, sir, they're a lot of 'em. As security, I'm always on my feet, always moving about."

"In general terms, then," Basil prompted.

With a dramatic gesture, Burgess inhaled and

scratched his pointy chin with a thin finger. "I left my flat at seven forty-five, checked in with my senior officer at the station, and began my rounds. I'm to help the passengers, but I also make myself of service to the railway police. I check doors and windows, make sure all the carriages and WCs are empty, look for unusual signs of tampering, that sort of thing. I chat with the porters and stewards, say hello to Mr. Tippet. Once the passengers board, I keep an eye out for trouble, any rabble-rousers or mischief-makers. It's not my job, per se, but like I said, I figure another set of eyes working for the railway police ain't gonna hurt."

"When did you check on the post office van?"

"I usually do that sometime before York. Then there are fifteen minutes where I eat my packed lunch. Usually, the mail sorters are so busy—work like bees, they do—hands moving so quickly they blur, no one speaking. It's kinda creepy if I do say so myself. They never pay me no mind, not a hello or a nod of the head."

"Except for today," Basil said.

"Today, they were frozen in horror—all gawking at the bag on the floor. I says, 'Is there a problem, gentlemen?' And Doring points at the bag before ducking his head into the rubbish bin and throwing up. I take a look and then run for Tippet." His eyes remained on Basil. "He tells me to get you, Chief Inspector."

"Mr. Burgess," Basil said as he stood. "We count on you to assist the constables present to ensure no one steps out of or gets into any of these carriages."

"Yes, sir."

Basil excused himself and returned to the first-class carriage in search of Ginger. He and Sullivan would begin their enquiries there after the inspector had completed his "inspection of the loo."

Ginger's search gave her a reason to question her fellow passengers—the suspects—if one was to be so bold.

"I saw her walk by," Mrs. Fisher said after Ginger had knocked and opened the glass door. "I supposed, at her age, she found it hard to sit for too long at one time. Poor thing, with that cane and in mourning to boot." The crow's feet around her eyes deepened and her eyes twinkled. "To think we're all going to be like her one day."

Ginger thought that was an odd thing to say in the company of her husband, even if the female sex did tend to outlive their male counterparts.

"Did you see where she went?"

The feather on Mrs. Fisher's forest-green, narrow-brimmed hat quivered as she shook her head. "I returned to the book I'm reading." She held up a copy of *A Passage to India*. "It's rather good. I've never been anywhere else in the empire. India sounds so exotic."

"Mr. Fisher?" Ginger prompted.

"I'm afraid I had my eyes closed. A short nap, you see," he replied.

Down the line, Ginger continued her enquires. The two businessmen hadn't seen Mrs. Simms, nor anyone else it seemed. By the time she reached Miss Dansby and Mr. Pierce's compartment, Ginger felt quite perplexed.

"Mrs. Griffiths," Irene Dansby said to the plain-looking lady beside her. "This is Mrs. Reed. She's the companion of my friend, Miss Gold."

Ginger extended a gloved hand. "Pleased to meet you. Are you also from York?"

The lady nodded, "I am." Her eyes, small behind round spectacles, were nondescript yet somehow familiar. Some people just had a common look. In fact, her clothing and general presentation bespoke of someone not accustomed to travelling first class. Ginger wondered at the relationship between the three York residents.

"An elderly lady joined us in London," Ginger started, "but she seems to have vanished into thin air. Her name is Mrs. Simms. She's wearing all black with a black veil over her face, and has a black cane. Have you seen her?"

Three heads shook at once. "Can't say I have," Mrs. Griffiths said. "Sounds to me as if she'd be hard to miss."

While some of the passengers had opened windows to combat stale air, others complained that the wind outside was too cold. Several decided to stretch their legs and stood in the corridor. Businessman Mr. Whitley was among them. He pointed a finger at Constable Mulgrew. "You can't keep us locked in here forever. Whatever happened in the post office van had nothing to do with us!"

Mr. Murray joined in. "You'll hear from my lawyer!"

Alarm flashed across Constable Mulgrew's face, and he raised his hands. "Calm down, gentlemen. Like I already said, your questions will be answered shortly."

"Please explain your intended meaning," Lady Pennington said curtly.

"Madam, it means you are required to be patient."

Ginger hoped Basil would return before a riot broke out. First-class passengers weren't accustomed to being inconvenienced.

CHAPTER SEVEN

Basil found Ginger engaged in conversation with PC Mulgrew. They stood by the door that separated the carriages. She smiled when he squeezed through the second door that connected the two carriages over the joined couplings. He loved how her green eyes sparkled like emeralds every time he walked into a room.

"How did it go?" she asked.

"Nothing earth-shattering. It appears that everyone was simply doing their jobs when the unfortunate event happened." Basil reached over to open a window. It gave one the illusion that the narrow corridor and cramped carriage had expanded. "The killer's motive must be to get the attention of someone in this carriage."

"No one here even knows what happened," Mulgrew stated.

"I want to tell them during the interviews. Reactions to news like that can be telling."

Ginger nodded. "Perhaps you'd like me to join you."

Knowing how captivating the smallest mystery was to his wife, Basil chuckled. She'd proven herself to be a tremendous benefit often during past cases. One tended to be less on one's guard in the company of a lady. "Your presence would be most welcome."

Mulgrew excused himself, proving himself to be intuitive enough to sense when a married couple wanted to be alone.

Ginger stared up at Basil in concern. "Have you got a temperature?" Her eyes darted to the opened window, and she wrapped her arms about herself and shivered.

Basil quickly closed the window.

"I do apologise, love. Sometimes I grow irrationally uncomfortable in small spaces."

"Like Haley," Ginger said with a nod. "You suffer from claustrophobia. You poor lambs."

Haley Higgins, a forensic doctor in training, was Ginger's very good American friend who'd recently moved back to Boston after the alarming news of her brother's death. Basil had grown fond of the sensible lady in the short time they had been acquainted.

Basil smelt a whiff of expensive French perfume before he caught sight of a beautifully made-up lady strolling along the aisle towards them. He sensed Ginger stiffen as they stepped apart. The lady ignored Ginger, keeping her sparkling blue-eyed gaze on Basil.

"You look to be someone of importance," she said to him as she reached out a gloved hand. "I'm Lady Isabel Pennington. You might recognise me from the opera house."

"Indeed. I'm Chief Inspector Reed. It's a pleasure to make your acquaintance."

"Reed?" Lady Pennington's gaze finally shifted to Ginger. "Are you related?"

"Married," Ginger said brightly. She threaded her arm through Basil's possessively, and Basil held in an amused smile. It wasn't only the male persuasion who marked their territory.

The wind outside whistled, but the lowering temperature wasn't solely responsible for the frosty atmosphere occurring now. He gave Ginger a reassuring look, and she released her hold.

"Is there something I can do for you?" he asked Lady Pennington.

"I understand there's been *a suspicious event,* and that no one is permitted to disembark. Perhaps you could telegraph for a taxicab? Surely, there must be a way off this contraption, even here in the middle of, well, wherever we are." Her eyes darted to Ginger reproachfully before smiling at Basil once again. She tilted her head and batted her eyes. "Chief Inspector?"

"I'd love to accommodate you, Lady Pennington, but as you said, there's been a suspicious event. I'm afraid this is a murder investigation."

CHAPTER EIGHT

It delighted Ginger to assist Basil with the first-class passenger interviews. Obviously, the passengers hadn't committed the murder—or rather, hadn't participated in the deposit of the victim's head onto the train—but she understood how prudent it was to find out if anyone had a connection to Mr. Wright. Perhaps someone could provide a clue that would help apprehend the person who had committed such a heinous crime.

She and Basil waited in the dining car, drinking tepid tea, as Constable Mulgrew ushered in the passengers, either in groups of two, if the persons were travelling together, or singly, if alone.

Mr. Claude Murray, a tall, willowy man, and his stockier companion, Mr. Robert Whitley, were the first to join them. They slid into the booth across from Ginger and Basil.

"I'm Chief Inspector Reed and this is my wife, Mrs. Reed. She'll sit in on the interview if you don't mind."

"If it suits you, it suits me," Mr. Murray replied with a shrug."

Mr. Whitley wasn't as nonchalant. "What on earth is going on? I demand to know why we're being held on board this blasted train?"

"I'm afraid there's been a suspicious death, and as a matter of form, the investigation necessitates that all persons who might've had access to the carriage in question be questioned.

"*What*?" Mr. Whitley said. "How could *we* possibly be involved?"

"It's quite probable that you're not," Basil said. "Like I said, it's just a matter of form."

"Well, do let's get on with it!" Mr. Murray proclaimed. "We have an important meeting in Edinburgh."

"Yes," Ginger said, "so you've mentioned. What kind of business are you gentlemen in?"

As if they'd forgotten she was there, both men looked at her for a moment in stunned silence.

"Please answer the lady," Basil prompted.

"We're in textiles."

Ginger and Basil shared a quick look. The victim was in textiles.

"And if we don't make this meeting in Edinburgh," Mr. Whitley added with exasperation, "we could lose a big contract,"

"Do you ever visit York?" Basil asked.

"York?" Mr. Whitley said. "I suppose on occasion if business demands it."

"Has business demanded it recently?" Ginger asked.

"We've made a deal selling wool to Luxembourg. What does any of this have to do with anything?"

Basil ignored the man's question and asked another. "Were you acquainted with Oscar Wright?"

"No, why would we be?" Mr. Murray said quickly.

Basil raised a dark, questioning brow. "Perhaps because he was a successful businessman in the textile industry?"

"Mr. Whitley?" Ginger asked.

"Yes, of course, we knew of him," Mr. Whitley returned. "He was our competition."

"Why?" Mr. Murray interjected.

"Are you admitting to knowing him now?" Basil said.

"Like Whitley said, we knew of him. Never made

his acquaintance." Mr. Murray's eyes opened as if something had dawned on him. "Don't tell me the old man died on this train?"

"I'm afraid it's more complicated than that," Basil said.

"How old was Mr. Wright?" Ginger asked.

"He's got to be in his eighties or nineties," Mr. Whitley said, then realising he had said too much, sat back, and pinched his lips together tightly.

"How would you know that if you've never met?" Ginger asked.

"He's been in the paper," Mr. Murray said. "Now, if we've answered your questions, are we free to leave?"

"I'm afraid you'll have to remain until all the interviews are completed," Basil said.

Whitley slammed the table. "That's preposterous! If we don't show up without word, we might lose the contract, and it'll be money lost due to railway incompetence."

"Would it help if you could send a telegraph?" Ginger asked.

Mr. Murray let out a sigh that was as long as his lengthy legs. "It would be better than nothing, I expect."

"Very well," Basil said. "Write out your message and give it to Constable Mulgrew. I'll ensure that it's given to Mr. Tippet, the engineer, and sent out immediately."

Ginger watched the men disappear and said, "I get the feeling those men knew Mr. Wright rather well. Why would they lie about that?"

"Excellent question, my dear."

CHAPTER NINE

The next couple to be escorted to the dining car were Mr. and Mrs. Fisher. The pair was equal in height and of average weight. Basil began with a similar introduction and a revelation of the death in the post office van.

Mrs. Fisher reached for the collar of her dress. "How dreadful."

"Was the person in question travelling first class?" Fisher asked sensibly.

"No. But we have reason to believe someone riding in this carriage may have known the victim."

Fisher nodded deeply as if that made perfect sense. "How can we help?"

"Are you acquainted with a businessman by the name of Mr. Oscar Wright?"

"He's a bigwig in York," Mrs. Fisher ventured, not

giving her husband a chance to speak at all. "Hobnobs with the Lord Mayor and the likes of him." She gasped. "Oh dear. Was he," leaning forwards she whispered, "*murdered?*"

"Why would you assume that?" Ginger asked. Though Basil had stated that a death had occurred, he hadn't mentioned that it was a violent one. She narrowed her eyes at the older woman suspiciously.

Mrs. Fisher huffed and waved a lace-trimmed handkerchief. "What other reason for this big charade? Uncoupling our carriage from the rest of the train, holding us like hostages. These mysterious interviews."

"You're quite right," Basil said, thinking that Mrs. Fisher was a lot brighter than what Basil had concluded on his first impression. "Mr. Wright has been murdered. Were you acquainted?"

Mrs. Fisher blinked in confusion. "I'm sure I don't know what you mean?"

Fisher finally interjected. "What he means, darling, is did we know Mr. Wright personally? Yes, we did. Up until recently York was our home. We've attended civic events. Though we've been introduced, I doubt he would remember us. He meets a lot of people, I'm sure."

"Where do you live now?" Ginger asked.

"A tiny village in Sussex," Mrs. Fisher said. "I inherited a cottage there."

"Is there a recent occasion that may have brought you and Mrs. Fisher into Mr. Wright's circle?" Basil asked.

"We protested with his factory workers. The working and living environments Mr. Wright condoned were appalling. They lived in worse conditions than most domestic animals."

Mrs. Fisher's round cheeks bloomed crimson as a thought took hold. "Oh my, do you think one of us killed him? You must! It explains why out of all the carriages on the train, ours is the only one to have been held behind!"

The rest of the interviews were unexciting and non-informative, and Ginger felt the fatigue that sitting for so long brings. Her teacup was empty, and there was no longer anything hot to drink available. She'd accepted an offer of a glass of water from the chef after he was interviewed.

"We must be getting to the end," Ginger said.

"This is the unglamorous part of police work, love," Basil said. "The worst is that we've not discovered anything new or substantial. Having met or known the victim isn't really much when one is dealing with a public figure."

"We've still got to see Felicia's friends, Miss

Dansby and Mr. Pierce, and their companion Mrs. Griffiths. Perhaps they can shed some light. And then there's Mrs. Simms. I do hope Felicia has rounded her up."

"Don't forget Lady Pennington."

"Quite right," Ginger said.

Miss Dansby and Mr. Pierce took their seats, and Basil proceeded with his introductions.

"Do you mind if I smoke?" Miss Dansby asked.

"Not at all," Basil said. He reached back to the table behind him, picked up the ashtray, and placed it in front of her. Miss Dansby elegantly removed a cigarette from a glossy cigarette case, and, as if from thin air, Mr. Pierce produced a silver lighter.

Miss Dansby inhaled deeply before exhaling a blue stream of smoke. "Felicia was helping to pass the time by regaling us with tales of your wedding."

"Tales?" Ginger asked, curious.

"How you lost Mr. Reed's ring and so forth, barely making it to the church on time. Such a lark if not a bit stereotypical." She tapped a short run of ash into the tray. "Felicia says she's your sister-in-law? So she's your sister, Chief Inspector?"

Ginger answered for him. "Felicia is the sister of my late husband. We still like to refer to each other as sisters."

"Oh, I see. She never mentioned."

Not such good friends, it seems, Ginger thought.

"Apparently, someone has died?" Miss Dansby said in between puffs. "Is that so uncommon on a train? I can't see why we must be inconvenienced."

"There's been a murder, Miss Dansby," Basil said. "We must interview anyone who might've possibly had access to the post office van, and that includes passengers in the carriage you were travelling in. Are either of you acquainted with Mr. Oscar Wright?"

"Indeed, I am," Mr. Pierce said. "My family's from York. I have a house there. Everyone knows who he is. Don't tell me *he's* been murdered?"

"I'm afraid so," Basil said.

"Wasn't he as old as the earth?" Miss Dansby said. "Why go to the bother of murdering someone who's bound to die of natural causes any day?"

Ginger had had that thought herself.

Mr. Pierce expressed the usual complaint. "What could this possibly have to do with us? We never visited the post office van. Certainly, someone would've seen us if we had. It's a fact easily corroborated."

"What line of work are you in, Mr. Pierce?" Basil asked.

The change in the direction of the enquiry caused the gentleman to stumble. "Uh, finance. Stocks and bonds and that kind of thing. It's very bully in the markets, my man. Do say you're investing. If not, I can help you out."

"Thank you for your offer," Basil said. "I'm fine for now. Mr. Pierce, when was the last time you saw Mr. Wright?"

"I'm friends with his son, Ronald, actually. We played a round of golf then had drinks at the Wright house a fortnight ago. Old Mr. Wright was there. A rare home visitation, I'm told. Like Miss Dansby has said, I can't see why anyone would bother."

"Does the untimely death of Mr. Wright hold any significance for either of you at all?" Ginger asked.

Miss Dansby stubbed out her cigarette. "I barely knew the man."

Mr. Pierce firmly shook his head. "Other than Ronald, I had nothing to do with Oscar Wright."

Ginger remembered the mousy-haired lady who had travelled in the same compartment with them. "How well do you know Mrs. Griffiths?" she asked.

"We only just met," Miss Dansby replied stiffly. "Now, I really must insist that I be permitted to claim my luggage and for travel to be arranged to take me home."

Basil stared back at her. "I'm afraid you'll have to wait like all the rest."

Basil waved over the constable who was standing

guard at the door and asked him to fetch Lady Pennington.

"Why don't I go for her," Ginger said. "I'd like to stretch my legs."

"Very well," Basil said. "It'll give me a moment to review my notes. But first," he took her wrist and pulled her close. "I think your groom deserves a kiss."

"I think he does too."

Fortified by Basil's affection, Ginger went in search of Lady Pennington. She really had to master these feelings of loss, going forwards without her title. She'd lived in Boston for years as a "Lady" and never dreamed of using her title then. She'd only grown fond of being "Lady Gold" since moving to London just a year ago. The difference was that in Boston, she didn't have to deal with the class system and the enormous social weight a title carries.

Lady Gold was no more. Ginger had Basil, and that was so much more valuable than a silly name.

Ginger paused at her compartment to speak to Felicia.

"The porter came for Boss to take him outside to do his business."

"Good," Ginger said. She'd made her request to the porter earlier on. There wasn't a platform where they were sidelined, which made it difficult for Ginger to do it herself. If someone had to inch down the attached steel ladder with a squirming dog in his arms, better the porter if he were willing.

She eyed the empty seat once occupied by the lady in mourning. "Still no Mrs. Simms?"

"I can't find her anywhere. She must've got off."

Ginger had to agree, but when? And how? Certainly, a lady of her age and lack of mobility would've had trouble without a platform. And even if she had managed the ladder, the Railway Police would most likely have seen her. Her very black wardrobe would be hard to miss."

"Are you doing all right, Felicia?"

"It's awfully boring. Why couldn't there be a handsome single man trapped here too?"

Ginger laughed. "If I'd known, I would've arranged it."

Felicia smiled. "I believe you would've! How are the interviews coming along? You must nearly be done, and then we can all get off this wretched train. It's terribly stuffy."

"You can open a window," Ginger said.

"And freeze to death? Listen to the wind. It's rattling the carriage. I'm almost fearful that it'll blow over!"

"I'm sure we'll be out of here before that happens. We've just got two interviews left."

Ginger continued to Lady Pennington's compartment and knocked gently on the glass door. Lady Pennington motioned for her to enter.

"Would you mind accompanying me, Lady Pennington? Chief Inspector Reed would like a short word."

Lady Pennington smoothed her frock, tugged on the hems of her royal-blue silk gloves that reached her elbows, and gathered her black satin Coco Chanel handbag. Protocol demanded that Ginger let the Lady go first. Ginger swallowed her distaste and followed her to the dining carriage.

CHAPTER TEN

Lady Pennington's nose was rather far in the air, Ginger thought as Constable Mulgrew escorted her through the double doors over the carriage coupling and to their table in the dining car. Her features softened when her eyes caught Basil's gaze.

"Please do tell me this dreary nonsense is to come to an end soon. I'm expected in Edinburgh this evening."

"Yes, well, let us get started then, shall we?" Basil said. "Are you a frequent traveller on the Flying Scotsman?"

"It depends on what you consider frequent, I suppose. Once or twice a month, perhaps? My mother is Scottish, you see, and that side of the family is rather more fun than my father's society crowd. He's Lord Pennington. I gather you've heard of him."

Ginger had only been resident in England for just over a year, but she'd become well versed in high society with the help of Ambrosia and Felicia. "Yes, he's quite influential," Ginger said. "I've met him once or twice."

"Wait a minute," Lady Pennington said, eyes widening with recollection. "Aren't you Lady Gold? With that red hair, I thought I recognised you." She laughed. "You gave up your title for love! I commend you, dear lady. I, for one, could never be tempted." She winked at Basil. "You must be quite a prize. Yes, perhaps if you had come into my life, I might've been enticed."

Ginger flushed with indignation. Did this lady have no scruples? Flirting with her husband right in front of her and during a murder investigation no less!

"Although," Lady Pennington said, staring back at Ginger. "You gained your title through marriage, didn't you? I remember reading about it in the society papers when you arrived from America. It seems fitting, in that case, Mrs. Reed, doesn't it, that you should naturally relinquish it."

Basil cleared his throat. "If you don't mind, Lady Pennington, I'd prefer if we kept to the point. Have you ever had the opportunity to become acquainted with an influential businessman from York known as Mr. Oscar Wright?"

"Of course. He and my father are friends. There's an age gap of twenty years or so, but quality cigars and a good single malt don't discriminate."

"So, your father and Mr. Wright met often?" Ginger asked. "Can you recall the last time?"

"Several months ago, I believe. Before his tiresome son had him committed to a nursing home. Mr. Wright's mind isn't as strong as it once was, and he failed to put up enough of a fight.

"Now you must divulge the reason for such queries? Has something happened to Mr. Wright?"

"Why do you ask that?" Ginger said.

"What other reason is there to be discussing him. He's not aboard the train, is he? I'm sure I would've spotted him in first class, otherwise."

"He's not on board," Basil began. "Rather, he wasn't a passenger on the train."

"Oh. All right then."

"There has been a death, and I'm afraid Mr. Wright is connected."

Ginger shot a sideways glance at Basil and bit her lip. That was one way to put it.

"Oh dear." Lady Pennington looked confused but not concerned. Her brows furrowed and she nibbled her lip. "You know, I believe I'm being followed. I'm not in danger, am I?"

"What makes you think you're being followed?" Ginger asked.

"Oh, it's just a feeling, like someone is always watching. You know how it is. Suddenly, for no reason at all, the hairs on the nape of one's neck are raised?"

Lady Pennington had just deftly turned herself from potential suspect to potential victim, Ginger thought. She glanced at Basil before saying, "You must be careful, Lady Pennington. Remain vigilant."

"Oh, I intend to."

"That will be all for now," Basil said, "but you'll have to remain on board for a while longer."

"Why? You can't just hold me here for no reason."

"We're in the middle of a murder investigation, Lady Pennington. The delay can't be helped."

"Very well. In that case, I'm travelling with a chest of some considerable value. I've been reassured by London and North Eastern Railway security, that my possessions would get to Edinburgh safely with me, but now, with this disruption, I'm concerned. I should like to inform my family so that they will know my luggage is arriving without me."

"I'm afraid the luggage van has also been detained."

"Whatever for?" She waved her gloved hand

dismissively. "I know, I know. It's a murder investigation. Poor second and third-class passengers, arriving without their bags."

"They will be notified when the luggage van eventually arrives."

"And my maid? She will wonder why she can't find me."

"Rest assured, Lady Pennington," Basil said. "Everyone has been notified about the circumstances."

"Of course." Lady Pennington batted thickly made-up eyelashes in Basil's direction. "Could you escort me to the luggage car so I can rest easy? Like I said, I've something of considerable value there."

"I'm rather busy at the moment, but Constable Mulgrew can assist you," Basil said, then gave instructions to PC Mulgrew. "Get one of the other constables to lead Lady Pennington to the luggage compartment and back to this carriage as soon as her concerns are alleviated."

"Thank you, Chief Inspector," Lady Pennington offered a bare hand for Basil to hold, before disappearing.

Ginger rolled her eyes. "There's no need to go gloveless. It's practically a refrigerator in here." Ginger wrapped her arms around her chest and shivered. "I mean, did she expect you to kiss her hand?"

Basil burst out laughing. "You're adorable when you're jealous."

"I'm not jealous!"

"Really?"

"Really." Ginger sniffed. "But I suppose I will have to get used to this type of distasteful display from shameless members of my own sex."

Basil kissed her cheek. "That road runs both ways, my dear."

Mrs. Griffiths was older than Ginger had first thought, perhaps in her late sixties, but spry with modern sensibilities of a lady half her age. Her short, well-styled hair was not yet completely grey. The skin on her face exposed her age with more lines than a younger counterpart. She had eyes that twinkled, which contributed to her sense of youth.

"It's a pleasure to meet you both," she said. Her voice was low and husky as if she'd spent most of her life smoking cigarettes, a possibility Ginger found hard to imagine. If the lady did indulge in what was still considered very much a gentleman's recreational pastime, she didn't ask permission to partake now. In fact, of all the passengers, Mrs. Griffiths seemed the least nervous to be questioned by Scotland Yard. Rather, she appeared enamoured.

"It's quite an honour to converse with you, Chief Inspector Reed. I've read quite a bit about the men of Scotland Yard. Sherlock Holmes to be precise. What a clever man! It must be so thrilling to outwit mischievous criminals."

Ginger glanced at Basil. Mrs. Griffiths did know that Sherlock Holmes was a fictional character, did she not? Nor was he of Scotland Yard, but rather a private detective. Ginger hoped the lady wasn't delusional.

Mrs. Griffiths chatted on. "My life isn't exciting at all. I'm so thankful for books. Aren't you, Mrs. Reed?" She patted her handbag. "I never leave home without something to read, especially whilst travelling on a train. Good thing, eh? Since today's journey has got rather long. In fact, I think you'll like this one—"

"Mrs. Griffiths," Basil cut in. "I'm afraid the news I have isn't from a storybook but is quite real. We've had a death on board. That is, there's been a murder..."

Mrs. Griffiths' palm went to her chest. "Oh my. A *real* murder!" Her lips worked like a fish gasping for air. "And *I'm* part of the story?"

"Is your final destination Edinburgh or York?" Ginger asked.

"York. To think, if the murder had happened after my stop, I would've *missed* it!"

"Yes, well," Basil said with far less enthusiasm.

"Did you ever meet Oscar Wright?" Ginger asked.

"Never had the privilege." She leaned in, her eyes gleaming with interest. "Is he—?"

"He is," Basil said.

"Ah." Mrs. Griffiths settled back into her seat. "I'm sorry to hear it. And at his age? He had to be close to ninety years old!" She chuckled. "He must have sold his soul to the devil, that one. Though apparently, he was in ill health. I read it in the paper recently." She stared at them with a sudden seriousness. "Nature was sure to take its course in due time. Violence at this point seems rather unnecessary, doesn't it?"

"Mrs. Griffiths," Ginger stated. "How well do you know Miss Dansby and Mr. Pierce?"

"I only just met them on the train today. A delightful couple. So nice of them to take pity on an old lady travelling alone.

CHAPTER ELEVEN

As he flipped through his notes, Basil ruminated over the information gathered from the interviews. "That's an interesting crew if I've ever seen one," he said. He hadn't expected the crime to be solved by the end of it, and he'd been correct.

Basil knew the young couple were friends of Felicia's, so he didn't want to step on any toes, but when there was a murder involved, he had to overturn every stone. "How well does Felicia know Miss Dansby and Mr. Pierce?"

"She only just met Mr. Pierce today," Ginger responded, "but apparently, Miss Dansby was a childhood friend from Chesterton."

"It would be prudent to ask Felicia a few questions later," Basil said. "Perhaps we should start with what we do know." He flipped to a clean page in his notebook. "Who of the first-class passengers lives or has lived in York?"

"Mr. Whitley has done business there," Ginger said.

Basil scribbled the name down and added, "And Mrs. Griffiths claims to live in the city."

"Mr. Pierce has a house there as well," Ginger added. "And the Dansby family moved there from Chesterton at some point."

"Righto," Basil said. "That's Mr. Whitley, Mrs. Griffiths, Mr. Pierce, and Miss Dansby. Now, who knew the victim personally?"

"Lady Pennington's father."

Basil started the new list. "Lord Pennington."

"Mr. Pierce, again," Ginger added. "He's friends with the son, Ronald Wright. No one else admitted to knowing him, though I suspect Mr. Murray and Mr. Whitley do."

Basil scribbled down the names, then said, "Only George Pierce is on both lists. I think we need to look into Miss Dansby's new fiancé a bit more." He was anxious to get off the dratted train himself. Fresh air and room to breathe would be most welcome. He wondered how Sullivan was doing in York.

"Why the lies?" Ginger asked.

"What do you mean?" Basil slipped his notebook back into his suit pocket.

"The businessmen and the Fisher couple lied about knowing the victim. I'm convinced that Miss Dansby and Mr. Pierce are being less than forthright, but I can't quite put my finger on what it is that's not lining up with their statements. Lady Pennington was more concerned about her luggage than the fact that a man had died."

There were many things Basil loved about Ginger. Her perception and ability to read people were among them.

"Sometimes people lie for no reason at all," Basil said. "A bad habit that formed over the years. Nervous people often don't think before they speak and can say something quite out of the blue, which hinders the investigation rather than helps it."

"Detective work is part puzzle solving and part luck," Ginger said.

"Yes, and sometimes it's hard to know which is which."

"Agreed!"

"By the way, has Mulgrew returned?" Basil asked.

"I presume Lady Pennington has him cornered," Ginger said.

"Yes, quite likely. I'm waiting for word from Sullivan. It would be useful to compare notes."

"Perhaps we should go and look for them."

"Who?" Basil asked.

"Lady Pennington and the young constable. He'll be quite helpless under her charm."

Basil chuckled. "The constable is a professional. I'm sure they'll return once they've accomplished their task."

"This constable is a *man*," Ginger returned, "but as you say, I'm sure he's fine. However, speaking of missing persons, we still haven't located Mrs. Simms. Whatever could've happened to her?"

"She must have disembarked somehow. Certainly, there is a logical explanation. Let's go and have another gander."

WITHOUT THE COAL driving the engine, there was no heat to be generated for the passenger carriages. Ginger wished she'd collected her coat, but instead wrapped her black embroidered cashmere stole more tightly about her shoulders. At least body heat shared in the small compartments created some warmth, but as they walked down the corridor to the luggage van, Ginger noticed that the temperature had dropped dramatically.

Ginger turned her chin towards her shoulder and said to Basil who followed closely behind her, "How long must we remain on board?"

"It depends on what we find in the luggage van."

The luggage van was full—stacks of suitcases, large chests, and even a collection of bicycles. It was attended by the guard, Mr. Carney, whose packed lunch was opened and abandoned on a lone wooden bench. Mr. Carney was at Lady Pennington's command.

"It's a small jewellery box. Brass trim. Locked. You assured me, Mr. Carney, that it would be secured and guarded."

"It is, madam. It's in the safe. I put it inside myself."

Constable Mulgrew stood by the door, hands clasped in front of himself.

"Anything untoward?" Basil asked him.

"Not that I can tell. Mr. Carney is opening the safe now."

Ginger raised a brow. "Any sign of Mrs. Simms?" Dead or alive?

"Who, madam?"

"Mrs. Simms," Ginger repeated. "An elderly lady in mourning who needed assistance to board the train. She's no longer in her seat, and I can't find her anywhere. Quite frankly, I'm concerned."

"That's it!" Lady Pennington's exhalation captured their attention and the subject of Mrs. Simms was put on hold.

With some effort, Mr. Carney carefully pulled the chest out from the large glossy-black Chubb safe.

"Are your fears assuaged, Lady Pennington?" Ginger asked.

Lady Pennington lifted the box, shook it lightly and frowned. She removed a set of keys from her handbag and unlocked the chest. Ginger couldn't see what was inside it, but the expression on Lady Pennington's face was one of undeniable shock.

"They're *gone.*"

"What's gone?" Basil said.

Ginger glanced at him with confusion. A diamond tiara with matching earrings sat elegantly on the blue satin lining.

"They're a Pennington family heirloom. Worth a fortune!"

"I don't understand," Basil said. "They appear to be accounted for."

"These are fakes!"

Oh, mercy.

"Are you certain?" Ginger said.

"Of course, I'm certain," Lady Pennington said scathingly. "I've known these jewels my whole life."

She glared indignantly at Ginger. "I checked them myself before leaving London. They were authentic. Someone exchanged them." Turning her full attention to Basil, she softened her tone. "You're the police. You must do something. I mustn't arrive in Edinburgh without the jewels. My father will surely have a heart attack."

"Are the exits secured?" Basil said to Mulgrew.

"Yes, sir. Immediately after the . . . uh . . . other incident, sir. No one has got on or off since the train stopped."

Except for Mrs. Simms, Ginger thought. She felt the sensation of a rock sinking into her belly.

Lady Pennington grew pale and collapsed onto the attendant's bench. "I feel faint."

Ginger went to her side. "Do you have salts in your handbag?"

"I don't need salts. A sherry will do."

"I'll fetch one from the dining carriage," Mr. Carney offered.

"Please do," Basil said, "then take a drinks trolley to first class. I'm sure they could use a drink too. And ask the chef to prepare some sandwiches to go with it."

Sensing a lack of welcome from Lady Pennington, Ginger returned to Basil's side.

"What are the odds of two crimes occurring on our wedding journey?"

Basil grinned crookedly and shook his head. "With you aboard, my dear, I can't say I'm surprised."

CHAPTER TWELVE

Lady Pennington is either an excellent actress or her distress was genuine, Ginger thought. The colour had drained from the lady's face, and she was dabbing small beads of perspiration from her brow. Mr. Carney returned with the glass of sherry Lady Pennington had requested, and she sipped it readily.

On Basil's instructions, Mr. Burgess and Mr. Carney stayed in the luggage van.

"I don't know how this could happen, sir," Mr. Carney said. His round eyes looked ready to spring from his face. "I put the case in the safe, just like the lady gave it to me."

"You may calm yourself, Mr. Carney," Basil said. "We'll get to the bottom of this."

Lady Pennington sighed in defeat. "My father's

going to kill me. He's always telling me not to take my expensive jewellery out of the house without proper security measures; tells me to wear the pastes instead. I never wear fakes, it's tacky, don't you think? If a lady is going to wear diamonds, they should be the real thing!

"Father doesn't really care about my jewels. These, however, aren't technically mine. They belong to the family. Father forbade me to take them, ever, so of course, they're the only ones I wanted to wear. Thankfully, Father doesn't read the London tabloids, so he never caught a picture with me wearing them." She glanced at Ginger. "Ladies like us can't help but end up in the society pages on occasion, can we?"

"Mr. Burgess," Basil said, turning to the conductor. "Please inform Mr. Tippet of this latest turn of events and have him send a telegraph to the station in York."

"Yes, sir."

"PC Mulgrew, I want a thorough search of this carriage. Ask one of the other constables to assist. Mr. Carney, please come with me."

Ginger loved it when Basil took control of a case. So masculine and strong. When he looked at her, she bit her lip to hold in the seductive grin that threatened. He asked her, "Would you accompany Lady Pennington to her compartment? I will join the two of you shortly."

. . .

Before claiming one of the empty seats in the lady's compartment, Ginger gathered two sherries from the drinks trolley and handed one to Lady Pennington.

"I can't imagine how this day could get worse," Lady Pennington said with a sigh.

"Well, you could be Mr. Wright . . ."

"Oh, yes. I apologise. So insensitive of me." She took two rather long sips in a row and then let out a long breath. "They're only jewels after all. I'm sure they'll be found eventually."

Ginger agreed. "It's beneficial to stay positive."

Lady Pennington drank her sherry in one long swallow and stared at the empty glass as if she could wish it full again. Her cheeks blushed with the rapid consumption.

"Tell me, Mrs. Reed, how did you and Mr. Reed meet?"

Ginger smiled. Why not entertain Lady Pennington with tales of her and Basil's romance? It was their honeymoon after all.

"We met on the SS *Rosa*, a steamship that travels from Boston to Liverpool."

"Did you know immediately that he was the one for you?"

"No. Not quite. But he was so dashing. And a fabulous dancer." Ginger recalled how they grew sweaty dancing the Charleston, and how much fun it was. It had been the first time in a long while she'd felt that kind of exhilaration.

"There was an incident with the Captain, and Mr. Reed headed up the investigation."

"And he let you assist?"

Ginger smirked. "Not voluntarily."

Lady Pennington laughed. "You are a lady who likes to go after what she wants, society be damned. We *are* alike in that regard."

Ginger sipped her sherry. If she wasn't careful, she'd end up liking Lady Pennington!

Within minutes, Basil joined them, and Ginger shifted down one seat. Constable Mulgrew and Mr. Carney waited in the corridor at Basil's request.

"If you would be so kind, Lady Pennington," Basil began. "Please run us through your whereabouts today."

The lady sighed dramatically. "Very well. I stayed the night at the Ritz Hotel. Rose early, had breakfast brought to my room. My maid helped me dress. She packed our suitcases, and we took a taxicab to the train station."

"Did you have any visitors at the hotel?" Ginger asked.

"None. I had all the socialising I could take after the opera. As much as I like attention, I also like to be alone."

"Did you ever leave your room without the diamonds?" Basil asked.

"No. I wore them to the event and didn't take them off until I was back in my room with the door locked. I immediately returned the jewellery to their case. This morning, I checked again, as is my habit, and they were safely in place."

"You're sure you had the real ones all along?" Ginger asked. "Well-made pastes can appear very convincing."

Lady Pennington shot Ginger a look of distaste. "I can spot fakes a mile away. I noticed these, didn't I?"

Ginger kept her chin up and held the lady's stare. "Yes, which leads me to wonder how you figured that out so quickly?"

"The real ones have a unique flaw in the large stone. If you don't know it's there, you don't notice it. Unless that is, you're a proper jeweller. But once you see it, you can't stop seeing it. You know how that is. These are not the same jewels I left my hotel room with this morning, I can assure you."

"Well, if the real jewels came on board, then they must still be on board," Basil said. He opened the door and spoke loudly. "Constable Mulgrew, search this carriage. I'm sure Mr. Carney will be more than pleased to assist."

Mr. Carney nodded his head. "Anything, sirs, anything."

Another officer interrupted with a knock. "Excuse me, Chief Inspector. Inspector Sullivan is back and would like a word."

CHAPTER THIRTEEN

Ginger and Basil sat with Sullivan in the dining car and filled the York inspector in on what they'd gleaned from the interviews along with this last crime.

"Crikey!" Inspector Sullivan said with a whistle. "When it rains it pours, don't it? Two major, seemingly unrelated crimes on one route. What are the odds of that?"

"Not high," Basil admitted.

"Do you think the theft was committed by a member of first class?" Ginger asked.

"It's possible," Basil offered.

"Could it be a misunderstanding?" Inspector Sullivan asked. "The fairer sex is known to be rather absent-minded." Then, as if feeling the heat of

Ginger's glare, he added, "Present company excluded, of course."

"Lady Pennington's recounting of her day and her knowledge of diamond quality is very convincing," Ginger said.

"I have to agree with Mrs. Reed, Inspector," Basil said. "I've learned to read people over the years, and I don't think she's lying. At least not about the diamonds."

"On my end, a Mr. Agar was conked on the head at the exchange apparatus in Doncaster. Not dead, thank goodness, but has sprouted a mighty turnip and I'm sure a bloody headache to go with it. It was his job to hang the mail bags on the apparatus and collect the drop off."

"Are you saying someone knocked him out and then replaced the mailbag with the head?" Basil asked.

"Appears so. Letters fluttering like loose chickens up and down the line. Unfortunately, Agar didn't see the scoundrel coming. He's in hospital now. Perhaps his memory will fill in over time."

"What about poor Mr. Wright?" Ginger asked. "Were you able to locate the remains?"

Inspector Sullivan pinched his lips together and shook his head. "We spoke to the nursing home where he lived—apparently his son ousted him out of his own home when he started having problems with, well, incontinence. They say Mr. Wright must've wandered off sometime after supper, though they didn't notice he wasn't at the home until it was time to put the patients to bed. They searched for him until two in the morning when they finally reported him missing to the police. Foot officers were out all night after that. This morning they are doing the rounds, asking neighbours and everyone else in the area if anyone saw him after eight p.m. last night, but there's nothing so far."

"And nothing that could be the murder weapon?" Ginger said. "Any idea what Mr. Agar was struck with?"

"My men have scoured the tracks going in both directions and so far, they've found nothing."

"What about his son, Ronald?" Basil asked.

"Funny thing, that. According to his secretary, Ronald Wright was at the opera in London last night."

"That's the event where Lady Pennington performed. Felicia's friends attended as well," Ginger said. "How coincidental."

Basil snorted. "I don't believe in coincidences. And I wouldn't be surprised if the murder and the robbery were connected after all." He referred to his notes. "Mr. Pierce, Miss Dansby, and Mrs. Griffiths live in York, and Mr. Whitley admitted to doing business there. Now, we find the victim's son was at the same social event as three other suspects."

"It's not unusual for passengers travelling on the Flying Scotsman from London to be from York," Inspector Sullivan said. "It's the only stop on the route."

"True," Ginger said. "But they happened to be on this particular route when these crimes took place."

"Quite right," Sullivan said. "Look here, would the two of you consider getting off in York tonight as well? Perhaps you'd like to take a look around."

Ginger stared longingly at Basil. The first night of their honeymoon was to be spent in Edinburgh at the Caledonian.

"It's up to you, love," Basil said.

As much as she wanted to head to the hotel, she couldn't see how either she or Basil would be able to relax with this mystery unsolved. Besides, any train they might yet catch would be a late one and the thought of travelling on into the night wasn't very appealing. "One night would be all right."

"First, we have to finish what we've started here," Basil said. "I'm going to see what Mulgrew has discovered. Ginger love, would you mind asking a few questions of our friends in first class? Perhaps Miss Dansby would confide in you about her time at the opera."

"Certainly," Ginger said. "I want to see how Felicia is holding up. Young people are quite shy of patience, I find." And of course, there was Boss. She was eager to ensure that he and the porter had returned, but she didn't speak that concern aloud.

"Ginger! Finally," Felicia said. "I was beginning to think you'd run off on your honeymoon somehow after all."

"Hello, Bossy!" Ginger scooped up her pet. "Are you being a good boy?"

Boss licked her chin, his little tail wagging happily at their reunion. Ginger removed a small jar of cooked steak cut into bite-sized pieces from her handbag and opened it to let him eat.

"There you are, old boy."

Ginger glanced up at Felicia who stared back with annoyance.

"Is something wrong?"

"I'd like to know what's going on. I feel completely abandoned!"

"I'm sorry, Felicia. We've run into another snag."

"Not another head!"

"No, a robbery. Lady Pennington's jewels, ones she apparently wore during her performance last night, are missing."

Felicia sighed. "I'm going to take my last breath on this train! I'll be old and grey with hair so long it will be creeping out of the window."

Ginger laughed. "Oh, Felicia! I do love your imagination."

"It's a lot more interesting than what's going on in this compartment. Please tell me we're to get off soon."

"We are. We'll be spending the night in York," Ginger said.

Felicia murmured, "Thank God for small mercies."

"Still no word on Mrs. Simms?" Ginger said, returning her attention to Felicia. "I'm quite alarmed by her continued absence." Whatever had happened to the elderly lady was most certainly not good. It wasn't like there was a place to get lost on four stranded carriages, even if one's mind had gone and one wandered off. The police officers stationed about would surely have seen her if she had indeed managed to get outside. And the weather was dreadful. A lady of that age and frailty wasn't likely to thrive out there.

Unless of course, Mrs. Simms wasn't a frail old lady. The black veil made it difficult to see her face. Her soft girth could be stuffing, her low voice could be a male falsetto. Ginger could think of two women and two men who could fit the bill according to their height: Mrs. Fisher, Mrs. Griffiths, Mr. Fisher, and the shorter businessman Mr. Whitley.

"I've checked for her everywhere like you asked," Felicia said. "It's like she's disappeared into thin air. Perhaps she *was* an apparition?" Felicia's voice was tinged with excitement. "I bet that's it. It would explain her fascination with death and funerals!"

Ginger smiled at Felicia's fancies. "I'm going to assume she was a flesh-and-blood person with a reasonable explanation for her disappearance."

"What's going on with everyone else?" Felicia asked. "Is Chief Inspector hubby about to make an arrest?"

"Sadly, no."

Ginger had glanced in on all the compartments on the way to her own. Lady Pennington nursed another sherry as she sat straight as a pole and stared ahead at seemingly nothing. Ginger wondered if the opera singer's concern for her reputation was merited. She wouldn't be surprised if news of the theft would, in fact, be a boon for her career. If Lady Pennington was aware of that, it could be considered motive. Perhaps the lady was a better actor than Ginger had given her credit for.

It seemed Mr. Fisher had given in to providence with head back and eyes closed. His mouth gaped open and when a snore was emitted, Ginger caught Mrs. Fisher giving him a sharp poke in the ribs with her elbow. He sorted himself out whilst she returned to her book.

Mr. Whitley and Mr. Murray gripped newspapers with tense, white-knuckled fists.

Mrs. Griffiths shared the compartment with Mr. Pierce and Miss Dansby. No one was speaking, but the expressions on the young couple's faces were tense and anxious. Mrs. Griffiths, on the other hand, seemed to be in happy spirits. Sitting in a seat next to the aisle gave her opportunity to catch the comings and goings of the others. A people watcher, Ginger thought, the kind who took in details.

"Have you had a chance to chat with Miss Dansby?" Ginger asked Felicia. "What does she have to say?"

"She's rather put out to be held up like this, but I should say, we all are. Our plans have been completely—"

"Derailed?"

"Very funny."

Ginger laughed. "My apologies, I couldn't resist."

CHAPTER FOURTEEN

Ginger moved Boss to the empty seat. "Please do excuse me, Felicia."

Felicia stared up with a stunned look on her face. "You're leaving me alone again?"

"You're not alone. Boss is with you."

"Very funny."

"I promise I shan't be long. I just want to check up on a couple of the passengers."

Felicia harrumphed, put Boss on her lap, and turned away from Ginger.

Ginger did feel bad for her sister-in-law and for her little dog. This day wasn't going well for anyone. She sighed as she stepped back into the corridor, then

knocked on the glass of the compartment occupied by Miss Dansby, Mr. Pierce, and Mrs. Griffiths.

Mrs. Griffiths nodded an invitation and Ginger

squeezed by to claim the seat opposite Irene Dansby. Felicia's friend was quick to bring up her grievances. "Please, Mrs. Reed, what is going on? Surely, as the chief inspector's wife, you must know something? It's outrageous how we've been kept here as if we were common criminals! Ask your husband to do something!"

"Miss Dansby," Ginger started gently, "I share in your frustration, as I, like you, am also kept here and cannot leave until permission is granted. The best we can do is surrender to the situation. I'm afraid things are out of my hands as they are out of yours."

"She's right, darling," George Pierce said. "We must stay calm."

Miss Dansby glared at her fiancé but didn't respond.

"Perhaps some conversation would help to pass the time," Ginger said. "I simply adore London, don't you? Tell me all about the opera last night."

"It was lovely," Miss Dansby said. "I know I should've rung Felicia, but I was with George. We're so recently engaged, I couldn't bear to share him. Oh, it was all very proper," she added quickly. "We each had our own room at the hotel."

Somehow Ginger doubted that but nodded as if she believed every word Felicia's friend was saying. "Did you have a chance to meet the stars of the performance?" Ginger asked. "Sometimes they invite people backstage."

"Not us," Mr. Pierce said. "Not this time."

"Not even to speak to Lady Pennington?"

Irene frowned and the beauty spot at the corner of her mouth seemed to grow larger. "Why would we? It's not like we know her. It's only providence that we're on the same train." She lowered her voice. "She's not as young as I thought, but then again, the stage is some distance away from the boxes, and they do wear a frightful amount of makeup."

"Do you visit London often?" Ginger asked. "I imagine you must like to come to the city to shop."

"They have shops in York, Mrs. Reed," George said stiffly.

"Felicia says you're on your honeymoon," Irene said, deflecting the subject from herself. "How sad to find yourself in this situation. Though Edinburgh is the last place I'd want to go after we're married. We're going to the south of France!"

George smiled, and his gaze lovingly washed over Irene. "I intend to give you whatever you want, my dear."

Ginger let out a soft sigh, frustrated that this conversation was getting her nowhere—not that she knew exactly what she'd hoped to find out. A quick glance about, and she caught the eye of Mrs. Griffiths. Ginger got to her feet.

"I'm sure we're soon to be released. Sit tight, Miss Dansby. Now, if you'll excuse me." She spoke to Mrs. Griffiths who had held her tongue this whole time. "Would you care to join me for a bit of air?"

Mrs. Griffiths responded to the invitation with enthusiasm. "You seem like a lady who notices things," Ginger said once they were in the corridor alone. "What are you noticing now?"

The older lady worked dry, wrinkled lips. "The group here is restless and resentful. None is a murderer, yet here they all are, held in a type of jail cell, under suspicion. The police are busy, not in here, clearly, but outside." She stared out of the window that had become fogged up and reached over to wipe it off. Indeed several officers were lumbering about.

"They're looking for something, or someone," she continued. "I suspect there is more going on than we've been told. You, for instance, have been on your feet more than most and visiting other carriages, whilst your friend, I believe I overheard someone mention she was your sister-in-law—"

"Miss Gold?"

"Yes, Miss Gold. Doesn't quite know what to do with herself. The middle-aged couple—I believe their name is Fisher—have been married for some time, and not happily I might add, though they're too set in the ways of the other to make any changes." She glanced over her shoulder and added, "Those businessmen are likely to kill someone if not set loose."

They had a clear view of Mr. Murray and Mr. Whitley's compartment from where they stood, and Ginger felt a growing sense of alarm. They were seated with arms crossed, lips tight, and necks bulging with blue veins.

"Oh dear, I see what you mean."

"Where's that drinks trolley?" Mrs. Griffiths said. "Someone should give them a stiff drink."

"Have you seen Mrs. Simms?" Ginger asked.

"Who?"

"An elderly lady dressed in black, veil and all, as if in mourning. I'm worried about her well-being."

"No. I haven't seen anyone who fits that description."

"Are you certain?" Ginger wondered if Felicia was on to something with her apparition theory.

Mrs. Griffiths shook her head. "Very."

CHAPTER FIFTEEN

"As a passenger, I've got luggage in the luggage van," Basil said, having return to the luggage van with Mr. Carney. "The procedure for my wife and me was simple—we dropped off our suitcases before walking down the platform to the first-class carriage." He had a single, if large suitcase, whereas Ginger had a stack of cases and hatboxes rolled to the luggage van by a porter.

By the number of items in the luggage van, Basil assumed several passengers had come with more bags than they could carry themselves. Ginger had also planned to bring her young maid, Lizzie, to help with whatever it was that ladies needed help with. Basil's father had a valet, but Basil couldn't see the point of having another man dress him. He was quite capable of dressing himself. Basil had convinced Ginger to leave her maid at home—he wanted to be alone with his new wife—and promised to arrange for help from the hotel.

Things didn't always turn out the way one planned.

"Mr. Carney," Basil continued, "walk us through your role as the attendant."

"Well, when a passenger arrives, I make a note of their name and their number of bags. I confirm that each bag is tagged properly and place it in one of the compartments, which are numbered so they're easy to find if necessary. I write the compartment number down and the passenger leaves."

Basil knew this from his own experience. "And with property of some value?"

"We've got two safes here, in the front of the carriage."

Again, Basil knew this to be true because Ginger had a small jewellery box deposited there.

"Who has the combination to the safes?" Sullivan asked.

"Just me," Carney said.

"Would you please open the safes, Mr. Carney," Basil said with authority, "and check with your register, that all the pieces are accounted for."

Basil, along with Sullivan and Burgess, watched

Carney carefully. "They're all here," Carney said, but this is rather interesting."

"What's that?" Sullivan said.

"This box in safe two is identical to the one belonging to Lady Pennington in safe one."

Basil took a closer look. Each was a steel box about a foot square and painted an unusual shade of green. Like sea foam.

"To whom does it belong?"

"Uh, a Miss Dansby, sir."

Basil raised a brow. "Are you certain?"

Carney showed Basil the register. Miss Dansby was listed as the owner of the piece described carefully on the page.

"It's not so uncommon for passengers to have identical luggage," Burgess said. "There are only so many types in circulation. We see it all the time."

"Yes, but how often do you see identical jewellery boxes where one has been subject to theft?"

Burgess swallowed hard again. "Well, when you put it that way."

"We need to see what's in that case," Sullivan said.

"Agreed," Basil said. "Mr. Burgess, would you please summon Miss Dansby? Oh, and Mrs. Reed, if you don't mind."

. . .

Basil caught Ginger's eye as she and Miss Dansby were ushered in, and trusted his wife would quickly catch on to the matter at hand.

"I suppose you are wondering why we've asked to see you, Miss Dansby," Basil began.

"Of course, I am! I'm extremely put out, and I'm beginning to feel that this is police harassment."

"Let me explain the reason," Basil continued. "We've discovered that you have brought a jewellery case on board that is an exact copy of Lady Pennington's."

"What of it? It's not a crime for one to have similar tastes to another."

"It all depends if one's similar tastes continue on to the contents. Would you please open your case?"

Irene Dansby blanched. Her fingers trembled slightly as one hand reached for the scarf around her neck. "I don't understand why I must."

"Lady Pennington's jewels have been stolen."

"And you think I took them? I demand to see my solicitor!"

"Are you refusing?" Basil asked.

Irene shot Ginger a fleeting glance, a plea. Ginger encouraged her with a nod.

"I c-can't. The key is lost. I was going to take the case to a locksmith later this week."

"I see," Basil said. Then to Burgess, "Please escort Miss Dansby back to her compartment."

"That's it?" Sullivan said, once Miss Dansby was out of earshot.

"If she refuses to produce a key," Basil said, "we'll have to open it another way."

"As much as I hate to hold those people any longer," Sullivan said, "I guess they'll have to wait until we can bring in someone who can pick open that case."

"Unless—" Basil said.

"Unless?" Sullivan prompted.

"Unless there's someone on board who could do the job."

"And you know someone like that?"

Basil grinned. "I do." He looked at Ginger. "Such a nice hat you have there, my dear."

Ginger laughed and removed two long, pointy hatpins.

Among other things, lock picking was a skill Ginger had acquired during her time with the British Secret Service in the Great War. However, it'd been a while since she'd been tasked with this kind of job, and it took her a mite longer than normal to manipulate the gear mechanisms in the small, but well-built lock.

When the lid finally popped open, silent awe filled the room.

"Blimey!" Mr. Carney said.

"Now I understand why Lady Pennington was so sure the others were fake," Sullivan said. "These are spectacular."

"Stunning," Ginger agreed. Even in the dim lighting of the luggage van, the pristine cut of the jewels reflected the light fantastically.

Mr. Burgess returned in time for Basil to give him another task. "Mr. Burgess, please ask Constable Mulgrew to escort Miss Dansby to the dining carriage.

Mr. Burgess returned a handkerchief to his pocket before saying, somewhat grudgingly, "Yes, sir."

"Is it my imagination," Ginger said quietly to Basil, "or is Mr. Burgess the nervous type."

"He has been mopping his brow rather frequently," Basil replied. "It's not exactly hot in here."

"Mr. Carney," Basil said, raising his voice. "How long have you been working on this route as the luggage attendant?"

"Three years, sir. Since before the train was christened The Flying Scotsman."

"And has Mr. Burgess been head conductor all that time?"

"Yes, sir."

Basil turned his back on Mr. Carney and spoke in a

lower tone to Sullivan. "We'll need your office to do a check on Mr. Burgess and Mr. Carney as well," he said. "Once I get to a telephone, I'll ring the Yard to see if they have anything on them."

Ginger turned to Mr. Carney and asked, "Did you notice anything unusual this morning whilst loading the luggage? Take some time to remember. The smallest oddity could be important."

"Well, let me see." Mr. Carney's brow furrowed as he concentrated. "Well, now that you mention it, someone bumped into Lady Pennington, and she dropped her handbag. I quickly picked it up, and that was the end of it."

"Was Lady Pennington's maid carrying her jewellery box or was it placed on the trolley with her other bags?" Ginger asked.

"It was on the trolley. On the top. Lady Pennington walked alongside the porter the whole time, with her hand resting on the box when the cart came to a stop. Very protective-like."

It appeared the lady didn't trust her maid.

"Even when she dropped her handbag?" Ginger pushed.

"Oh, well, there might've been a moment there, I suppose."

Ginger glanced up at Basil. "Time to swap one for the other?"

"Indeed."

"I'm staying here with Mr. Carney and the jewels," Sullivan said, "until we can get them reunited with their owner. I'll send word to Lady Pennington that they've been found."

"I'm sure she'll be relieved," Ginger said.

Basil asked PC Mulgrew to escort the first-class passengers into the dining carriage. Low murmurs erupted into loud protests the second Basil and Sullivan entered.

"Are you going to release us now?"

"We demand an explanation!"

"You've got no right holding us like this!"

Sullivan waved meaty palms. "Calm down, everyone. A new situation has arisen. I'll let Chief Inspector Reed explain."

Basil looked out at all the eager faces, letting his gaze rest on Ginger who'd found Felicia at a table and had slipped in beside her.

When their eyes met, he was relieved to see one reasonable and supportive person. His lips pulled up slightly, a small smile just for her, before he focused on the whole group with a tone and look far more serious.

"If you haven't yet heard, we've discovered a second crime on board this section of the Flying Scotsman." He paused to take in the myriad expressions. Disbelief tinged with frustration (Whitley and Murray); surrender (Mr. and Mrs. Fisher); and in some, amusement (Mrs. Griffiths, for one). Basil imagined that many people had lived out their days without ever having an exciting day in their lives until this one.

"Another murder?" Whitley called out. "You can't be serious."

"No, not a murder," Basil said, but his thoughts went to the missing Mrs. Simms and wondered if there was yet another body to be soon discovered. "A theft. Precious jewels belonging to the Pennington family estate. I know we're all anxious to be ushered off this carriage—and rest assured, a bus is on its way—so to save time, may I have a show of hands, everyone who attended Lady Pennington's opera performance in London last night?"

Slowly, hands reached up as heads spun like owls to witness the performance. Four hands went up belonging to the Fishers, Miss Dansby, and Pierce.

Basil scoured the rest of the faces. Lady Pennington was a big draw, and she had had her jewels stolen. Basil expected more. "Is that all? Rest assured, you are all being investigated, and the truth will be discovered."

"Blimey!" Whitley spat out. Reluctantly, his hand

went in the air, along with Murray's. "I suppose we'll have to stay behind when the others go?"

"I'm afraid you're right," Basil said. "We'll proceed as quickly as we can. You may return to your compartments until the bus arrives. And, Miss Dansby? Please stay behind for a few moments once the others have gone."

CHAPTER SIXTEEN

Irene Dansby looks a sight, Ginger thought, as she and Basil joined her.

"Someone bumped into Lady Pennington whilst she was preparing to have her luggage loaded," Basil said. "Was it you, Miss Dansby? Or are you working with someone?"

"Like I said before, I don't know what you're talking about."

"Lady Pennington's jewels were found in your case," Ginger said.

"You opened it?" The colour of Miss Dansby's eyes darkened with panic. "Isn't that against the law?"

"Not when a crime is suspected," Basil said. "Now, is someone working with you, Miss Dansby? Or did you cause a diversion yourself? Mr. Carney has given evidence that a disturbance large enough to divert his attention from his task, happened whilst you and Lady Pennington were standing in the queue to register your belongings."

"You should ask Mr. Carney then," Irene said. "He must've swapped the pieces. Certainly, it happened without my knowledge."

"Did it?" Ginger said. "If Mr. Carney was involved, he had to know about the jewels in each of your bags somehow? And since you, only, would know for sure. . ."

"Or perhaps it was Mr. Pierce who packed the case," Basil offered.

"Stop, stop! I implore you."

"Was it Mr. Pierce?" Ginger asked.

Fear flashed behind Irene's eyes. "No. It was me. I acted alone. Created the disturbance, made the exchange. I did it myself."

Basil leaned back against his seat, his eyes never leaving Miss Dansby. "You're confessing to manufacturing pastes, arranging possession of a case that is the duplicate of Lady Pennington's, creating a distraction, and making the exchange all on your own?"

"I am. And if there hadn't been that rotten murder to stop the train, I would've got off at York, and Lady Pennington would've been none the wiser until she returned to her home in Edinburgh."

"It's rotten luck," Ginger said. "But, why, Miss Dansby? Your family is well off, surely?"

Irene shrugged a slender shoulder. "Just to see if I could. I was bored, you see. This was a challenge."

"Very well," Basil said. "Miss Irene Dansby, I am arresting you on suspicion of theft."

Irene gaped. "But I didn't actually steal them! They're still on board this train and easily returned to Lady Pennington."

"The intention is there," Basil said. "We'll let a jury decide your fate."

"Unless," Ginger said, "you want to tell us the truth."

"All right!" Irene said. "I just need a moment to think."

Ginger inclined her head. "The truth should be rather straightforward."

"Could I please have a glass of water?" Irene coughed politely into a handkerchief.

Basil rose from his seat to retrieve the water from the kitchen's pantry.

Ginger leaned in and sputtered. "If you tell the truth now, the courts may go easy on you. If you lie again, all hope of that is gone."

Basil returned, and Irene made a performance of taking a long drink. Ginger could see the wheels turning behind Irene's heavily made-up eyes.

Calculating her next move, Ginger thought.

"Thank you," she said, setting the glass down on the table that separated them.

"Are you ready, Miss Dansby?" Basil asked. "And please don't insult our intelligence. As bright as you might be, I don't think you pulled this off alone."

Irene snorted. "I was approached by someone, and a deal was offered. The idea and execution came from this secondary party. We were offered a generous cut once the jewels were sold."

"We?" Ginger said.

"I," Irene said quickly. "I mean I. Anyway, as I told you, there is a secondary party."

"Someone on this train?" Basil said. "George Pierce perhaps? You know we will interrogate him until he confesses."

"Fine. George and I were approached. And not only us. There is one other."

"Who?" Ginger asked. "Is he or she on this train?"

Irene nodded. Now that she had given herself and her fiancé up, it seemed she was willing to spill the beans on the others. "It's Mr. Burgess."

Ginger glanced at Basil. Mr. Burgess made sense. He had worked on the route for years, probably looking for a way to get up in the world.

"Not Mr. Carney?" Ginger confirmed.

Irene scoffed. "That bumbling idiot? No."

"Tell us exactly how the theft was to be executed?" Basil said.

"Our task was to learn as much as possible about Lady Pennington and the family heirloom jewels. Where she went, how she dressed, her performance schedule, that sort of thing."

So, Lady Pennington hadn't been paranoid. She had, indeed, been followed.

"We learned about her luggage brand and how she transported her jewels. Quite carelessly, I would add."

Irene Dansby paused to take another quick sip of water before continuing.

"George and I went to her performance last night—we needed a reason to come to London, so why not? We stayed at the same hotel, followed her to the station the next day. We needed to make sure she brought her jewels on board.

"George distracted Lady Pennington. At the same time, Mr. Burgess distracted Mr. Carney. I made the exchange. Like I said before, we were to get off at York before anyone knew any better. Such blasted bad luck someone chose this train to knock someone off."

"Yes," Basil said wryly. "The man's murder is such an inconvenience to us all."

"So, I've told you the truth," Irene said. She leaned back and crossed slender arms. "You promised the courts will go easy on me."

"We'll put in a good word," Basil said.

"Who approached you in the first place?" Ginger asked. "Who's the mastermind?"

"Some nutty, odd-looking old lady. I laughed at first, thinking she was off her rocker when she called us together for tea. But," Irene sighed, "obviously, she convinced us."

"Who was the lady?" Basil asked.

Ginger answered. "Mrs. Simms."

Irene stared back in surprise. "How did you know?"

Felicia almost sprang on Ginger when she returned to her seat in the passenger carriage.

"What's going on, Ginger?"

Boss looked up drowsily then promptly closed his eyes and fell back to sleep.

"Where's Irene?" Felicia demanded.

"I'm afraid my news isn't good, love," Ginger murmured. She sat and lifted her drowsy pet onto her lap. "Irene has confessed to the attempted theft of Lady Pennington's jewels."

Felicia blinked back in shock at the news. "I can't believe it! I thought I knew her."

"I'm afraid it's true. Mr. Pierce and the railway

security chap, Mr. Burgess, have all been implicated. Along with Mrs. Simms."

"Ginger, you've no shortage of shocking news. Mr. Pierce must've compelled Irene somehow. Blackmail, perhaps. But, Mrs. Simms, as well? It just doesn't make sense. Have you located the morose old lady?"

"No, she's still missing, but at least now you can rest assured that we weren't entertaining a ghost earlier," Ginger said.

"Unless a ghost had entertained Irene and the others."

"Now, why would a ghost be interested in jewels? It's not like an apparition can wear them to a ball."

"True, but it could just be a matter of spite," Felicia said, as she smoothed out the folds of her chemise day frock and adjusted the large velvet ribbon at her hip. "Ghosts can hold a grudge, I've heard."

"From whom?" Ginger patted at her red bob, having removed her hat when the pins came out. "Really, Felicia, I'm concerned about the company you keep."

"Well, you can't blame me. I thought Irene Dansby to be entirely suitable."

Ginger sighed. She'd thought the same thing only hours ago.

"I hope this means we can get off this wretched

train now," Felicia said. She shifted awkwardly in her seat. "My back and behind can't take it anymore."

Ginger laughed. "I believe the bus is on its way."

Felicia folded her arms across her chest. "Jolly good."

"I'm going to visit the lavatory," Ginger said. She intended to do her own search for Mrs. Simms, and she didn't want Felicia dragging along. "I'll be back shortly. Please keep an eye on Boss."

Ginger shifted Boss off her lap, bent to retrieve her handbag, and took a moment to search around the seat where Mrs. Simms had sat. She found nothing untoward. The lady had entered the carriage from the south end, and Ginger took extra care to scan the aisle and steps around the door. There was the usual amount of dirt that could've been tracked in by anyone but nothing else out of the ordinary.

She hadn't seen Mrs. Simms attempt to reach the north end of the carriage or make her way to any of the other carriages, and her enquiry earlier proved that none of the other passengers had either.

The lavatory was small with just enough room for a larger person to turn around uncomfortably. There were a small sink and mirror, but the lighting came from a small window, too small for a normal-sized person to escape through.

Something on the floor beside the toilet caught

Ginger's eye. With a gloved hand, she retrieved it—the rubber tip found on the bottom of canes for grip. Ginger rechecked the window. It opened easily. A quick way to dispose of a cane should one care to be rid of such a thing.

CHAPTER SEVENTEEN

Two buses arrived, one for passengers and one for the police. The police bus was loaded first.

Once Miss Dansby, Mr. Pierce, and Mr. Burgess were led off the carriage wearing handcuffs, the other passengers disembarked. The winter winds blew cold, and storm clouds gathered angrily overhead.

"One case solved," Basil said, "but still another beckons."

Ginger showed him the rubber tip she'd found in the lavatory. "I think Mrs. Simms was someone else in disguise."

"Another woman on board?" Basil said. "Mrs. Fisher? Mrs. Griffiths, perhaps?"

"Or a smaller man," Ginger said. "Mr. Fisher would also qualify as would Mr. Burgess and Mr.

Whitley. 'Mrs. Simms' wore a thick veil and spoke with a rather low voice for a woman."

"Our thief?" Basil said. "That would be a strange connection between the two cases.

"At any rate, I don't think Mrs. Simms exists."

"Then why the performance?" Basil asked. "And what happened to the cane?"

"I believe the cane was thrown out of the lavatory window," Ginger said. "As for the performance, maybe 'Mrs. Simms' wanted to see if the robbery was a success, but when the train was stopped, she feared her alias would be discovered."

"I'll get some men to search the tracks for evidence."

Constable Mulgrew approached. "We've got everyone out, except for you two and Miss Gold."

"What about Inspector Sullivan?" Basil asked.

"He's gone with the accused, sir. We have an extra motorcar if you'd rather travel separately from the other lot.

"That would be splendid," Basil said.

Ginger bundled up in her fur-trimmed wool coat and fastened the over-sized buttons that ran fashionably at an angle. She pinned on her hat, wrapped her scarf snugly around her neck, and braced herself against the icy wind.

"I don't know what we were thinking, going north

in October for our honeymoon." She glanced up at Basil.

Basil stretched an arm over her shoulders for warmth. "To think we could be sipping fruity cocktails on a beach in Savona."

"Oh, mercy! Now I really regret it. For some reason, the picture of a castle on the hill and miles of craggy shore seemed *so* romantic. Now we're spending our honeymoon in York, of all places."

"With me," Felicia broke in. "Now that my good friend has been apprehended, I really am going to play gooseberry."

Ginger laughed as she slid into the back seat beside the solemn girl. "And a most lovely gooseberry you are!"

THE BUSLOAD of delayed first-class Flying Scotsman passengers entered the historic city of York after the last train had left the station. Basil was pleased with the misfortune of its occupants. It gave him more time to study the suspects—after all, any one of them could easily be mixed up in the murder given that the head had been deposited on board for a reason. It was up to him to discover what that reason was.

He and Ginger had opted to stay in the same hotel as the others though Sullivan had been kind enough to offer them something a little classier. Ginger had answered before he even had a chance, saying they must stay with the others. Her drive to solve this case was as strong as his was. She could've been moping about not having a proper start to their honeymoon, and the fact that she wasn't made Basil love her even more. At least, they'd had two nights alone together in the bridal suite at Brown's Hotel in London.

"I confess I was a mite worried that the train ride might feel rather anti-climatic," Ginger said as they readied themselves in their room for dinner. "No need to fret about that now."

"Indeed not."

"I am sorry for Felicia. She's so concerned about impinging on our time together, and now her close friend has been arrested. Her plans have been ruined."

"Rather bad luck," Basil said. "Maybe she'll meet a gentleman in the hotel dining room that will take her mind off things."

"Aha!" Ginger tugged on his sleeve. "You are a hopeless romantic. I knew it!"

Basil grabbed her by the waist and pulled her close. "I am for you, my love."

A knock on the door interrupted a rather delectable kiss. Basil stifled a groan.

"Ginger?" Felicia's voice came from the passage. "Sorry to disturb you."

"Not at all," Ginger called out. She opened the door to Felicia's solemn countenance.

"I'll meet you downstairs," Felicia said. "I just wanted to let you know."

"Please would you find a table for us?" Ginger asked.

"Are you sure you want to sit with me? You must be just sick of my presence already."

"Don't be silly. It's not like we'll be alone in the dining room anyway."

"We're going to people watch," Basil said to Felicia. "You enjoy that game, don't you?"

"Well, yes." Felicia allowed a smile. "I'm rather good at it too."

"Fantastic," Basil said. "You can play with us then. Maybe someone will reveal a clue."

"You'll let me help with the investigation?" Felicia said, her mood now brightened.

"You can help by observing," Ginger said. "It's an important detective skill."

Basil felt a sense of satisfaction in having turned the mood around. He liked Felicia, and for the most part, enjoyed her company. However, there was enough rain coming down that they didn't need a cloud hovering over their table at the restaurant as well.

CHAPTER EIGHTEEN

Founded by the Romans, York was a walled city encircling York Castle. It became a significant trading centre due, in large part, to the River Ouse, which ran through it. The headquarters of the North Eastern Railway were situated there along with—much to Ginger and Felicia's delight—two major chocolate manufacturers.

Basil was just glad to be off the train. Too much time in cramped quarters made him feel as if he were wearing a suit a size too small.

As Basil had hoped, the suspects had gathered in the hotel restaurant for a late dinner as well. Mr. and Mrs. Fisher sat by the window. Wearing his customary scowl, Mr. Doring sat alone in the bar area. Mrs. Griffiths, also alone, was seated in one of the corners with her back to the wall. Ginger wondered why she hadn't gone home, but then again, the spry elderly lady was probably too curious to leave the drama just yet. Mrs. Griffith's brow shot up when her gaze latched on to Basil's, a sign of solidarity as if to say she was on the lookout for the perpetrator too.

Absent, of course, was Lady Pennington. Basil had been informed by Constable Mulgrew that she had taken up Sullivan's offer to stay at the Grand Hotel and Spa about a mile away.

"Isn't this quaint," Ginger said, as they were seated.

"I hope the weather breaks tomorrow," Felicia said. "Then we can meander through all the narrow medieval passages—"

"Snickelways," Ginger said, interrupting. "That's what they're called, aren't they? Simply charming little pathways."

"Yes," Felicia replied. "I've heard they've turned some of the old butchers shops into dazzling fashion and jewellery shops. We simply must take a gander."

A waiter appeared at their table with a notepad in hand. "Sir, ladies, would you like something to drink?"

"I'd like a daiquiri," Felicia said. "It's an American cocktail." At Ginger's look of surprise, she added, "I've heard you mention it."

"I thought Americans didn't imbibe," the waiter said.

"It's against the law to drink," Ginger said. "But, believe me, Americans are still imbibing."

"*Cocktails* are served in the cocktail lounge," the waiter said rather snootily.

"Oh," Felicia pouted. "I'll have a glass of chardonnay then. And be quick about it as I've had a very trying day."

Ginger nodded at Basil, and he said, "Please make it a bottle."

The waiter spun on his heel and returned to the bar.

"We want to make his job easy, Felicia," Ginger said. "He'll be more inclined to cooperate should we want to ask questions."

"Of course, you're right," Felicia muttered. "I hope I didn't bungle it up. I'll be extremely kind and friendly when he returns."

When the waiter returned with a chilled bottle and three wine glasses on the tray, Felicia was all smiles and fluttering eyelashes. "Forgive me for earlier," she said. "My very close friend was recently arrested. It's so upsetting."

The waiter stared back. "Were you on that train where a robbery was daringly prevented? It's in the evening papers."

Daringly prevented? What exactly had the rags written, Basil wondered. He waited to see if the waiter would bring up the murder and was satisfied when the man didn't. It could be disastrous for the investigation if word got out too soon.

They placed their meal order: medallions of beef bordelaise for Ginger; roast lamb with mint sauce for Felicia; and mutton in cream sauce with rosemary-covered baked potatoes for Basil.

The waiter's expression was stony, but Basil got the feeling that steak and kidney pie was more to the liking of what the average customer ordered there. He wouldn't doubt if the kitchen in the back simply rang up the kitchen at the Grand Hotel and placed the order. The menu prices would support that.

"So, Felicia," Basil said wanting to humour her, "What are your impressions of the characters in the room?"

"Well—" Felicia's eyes scanned the dimly lit restaurant. "Mr. Doring likes his own company. He hasn't lifted his eyes from his drink since we arrived."

"Yes," Ginger added. "He's nervous about something, yet finds comfort from his perch on that stool."

"It could be that he's been seriously rattled and just needs a drink," Basil said. "Most people would be with the shock of the discovery of a dismembered head."

"Mr. and Mrs. Fisher have a marriage of convenience," Ginger said. "They seem perfectly content to sit together without speaking."

"Yes, but did it start that way?" Felicia asked. "They appear to be in their fifties, wouldn't you say? After thirty years of marriage, I doubt there's anything left to talk about."

"Unless a theft and a murder happened on your journey," Ginger said. "Surely, that's a reason to talk."

"Good point," Felicia said. "Perhaps the habit of keeping to oneself is simply too ingrained."

Basil smiled as the sisters debated the character of strangers. He agreed with their assessment of the Fishers. If they were involved in either crime in any way, it was possible that they weren't even married. In fact, there was a look of similarity about them. Something was rather *fishy* about the Fishers.

"Do you think the Fishers might be siblings," he said, "and not a married couple?"

Ginger stared at the strange duo. "There's something in the eyes. They could be cousins. It's not so uncommon for cousins to wed."

"She would be Miss rather than Mrs.," Felicia said, "if they weren't married."

"Not necessarily," Ginger said. "Many ladies of a certain age take on the title of Missus, especially if they work in service. Our own Mrs. Beasley is an example."

The meals arrived and after a round of *bon appétit!* they began to eat. The mutton wasn't the best Basil had ever had, but it wasn't the worst either. Ginger and Felicia muttered similar sentiments.

"Mrs. Griffiths is a strange one," Felicia said after a few bites of lamb. "She's like a hawk, eyes everywhere."

"She seems to be fascinated with our table," Ginger said.

"More amused than distressed by the events of the day," Basil added. "She said she was from York. I wonder what brings her to this restaurant tonight."

"She probably spends a good amount of time at home alone and bored," Felicia offered. "One can't blame her for finding relief in this kind of diversion. I'd do the same thing if I were her."

Ginger sipped her chardonnay then added, "She's the curious type, the kind who wouldn't want to miss anything scandalous."

"What are your plans now?" Basil asked Felicia.

"I suppose I'll return to London. Once Grandmother gets wind of this, she'll be arranging for a telegraph to be sent and demanding my return anyway."

Basil smirked. The Dowager Lady Gold was a force to be reckoned with to be sure—and the only lady Felicia had ever known as a mother figure. They had a complicated relationship, one that Basil never hoped to figure out.

"There's not much for you here now that Irene's been arrested," Ginger added.

"I should go to her," Felicia said. "She's my friend."

"She and Mr. Pierce will likely be out on bail soon," Basil said.

Felicia dabbed her mouth with her cloth napkin. "Perhaps I'll stay awhile then."

"Do you think that's a good idea?" Ginger's beautiful brow furrowed in worry. "I know she's a friend, but she did commit a serious crime. You wouldn't want to get implicated in any way."

"I shan't!" Felicia said with a laugh. "One of Scotland Yard's chief inspectors is practically my brother-in-law!"

CHAPTER NINETEEN

The next morning, Ginger and Basil took a taxicab to the York Police station in search of Inspector Sullivan. They were directed to a small office behind the reception area and found the scruffy gentleman there. It was the first time Ginger had seen the man without a hat and she noticed a rather large balding spot on the top of his head.

"Yes, hello," Inspector Sullivan said. "I expected that you would show up here today." He reached for a cigarette case, offered it to Basil and Ginger who both shook their heads, before taking a cigarette for himself and lighting it.

Basil pulled out a chair for Ginger and took a second one for himself. "Is there anything new to report?"

"I've sent out men to scour the railway line again

this morning. Could be they missed something yesterday. It was getting dark and hard to see by the time they got out there." He let out a billow of smoke from the side of his mouth. "I don't expect they'll find anything, but I like to be thorough."

"I suspect they'll find a black cane with the rubber tip missing," Ginger said.

Inspector Sullivan blew smoke from the side of his mouth. "Is that so?"

"We have reason to believe the mourning passenger who called herself Mrs. Simms was someone else in disguise."

"That would explain why she disappeared into thin air," Inspector Sullivan said. "But what happened to her clothes? All black you say?"

Ginger nodded, "Yes, widow's wear. The person must've carried on an empty handbag or holdall. He or she could've simply removed the black clothing, having their day clothes already on underneath."

The inspector conceded. "I'll make sure the men keep their eyes open for a cane."

"Make sure they wear gloves," Ginger said. "Finger prints."

Inspector Sullivan glared at her as he tapped ash into a tray. "I know how to do my job, Mrs. Reed."

"My wife means no offence," Basil said. "She just wants what we all do - to solve this case."

Ginger smiled at her husband appreciatively.

Inspector Sullivan shrugged.

Basil continued, "I'd like to visit the victim's house today, along with the post office where the mail bag came from—"

"It's forty miles to Doncaster."

"Yes, I'm aware of that," Basil said. "I'd also like to speak with the unlucky bloke who got knocked out at the drop off point."

"Doncaster Hospital. Nine stitches, the poor chap." Inspector Sullivan squashed his cigarette butt until the red ember died to grey. "I sent a man to make those rounds. Hospital last night, post office this morning."

"And?"

"Not anything of note. Perhaps you'll have better luck." To Ginger he said, "Your sister, she's gone back to London?"

"I wish that were the case," Ginger said. "No, she insisted on going to Miss Dansby's house and offering her support. They are childhood friends."

"I remember that fact now." He leaned in over his desk. "Just how close are they, would you say? Close enough that Miss Dansby would confide in her? I hate to say it, but we'll have to investigate Miss Gold, as a matter of form."

Ginger was indignant. "I can assure you she had

nothing to do with the theft of Lady Pennington's jewels."

"All the same. I know how the ladies like to talk. I'm sure she must know something."

Ginger pursed her lips as she silently kicked herself. She should've insisted that Felicia got on the train to London right after breakfast.

Basil took her hand. "It's only a matter of form."

"Of course."

"I don't have to remind you, Chief Inspector Reed, to keep an open mind. Or should I speak to the chief constable."

"I can assure you, Inspector Sullivan," Basil said stiffly, "that I will continue to operate with the utmost professionalism. Now, if you've nothing else, Mrs. Reed and I will begin our enquires."

"Certainly," Inspector Sullivan said, leaning back in his wooden office chair. "It is mighty unusual for a police officer to take his wife along on his interviews."

"True," Basil said. "But my wife isn't a run-of-the-mill wife."

Ginger jutted her chin into the air. "I'm a private investigator."

"Yes," Inspector Sullivan said dismissively. "You mentioned that on the train."

CHAPTER TWENTY

"I don't remember Inspector Sullivan being so rude and condescending," Ginger complained, feeling quite annoyed as they left the police station. "He was like a different person."

"I doubt he got much sleep last night," Basil said.

"I noticed the dark circles around his eyes too," Ginger said. "Still, it's no excuse for boorish behaviour."

"Indeed," Basil agreed.

"I won't let the man get under my skin," Ginger said, realising that Inspector Sullivan's behaviour had already provoked her. She took in a slow breath and released it. "Where do you want to begin?"

"Doncaster," Basil said. "There has to be evidence about the murder somewhere in that area."

Basil hired a motorcar. (Ginger could hear Haley's

voice in her head. "You hire people and rent things!" They often laughed at the differences between British and American culture.) It was painted a glossy black, it had a high box-like carriage and a long bonnet fronted with round, headlamps that looked like enormous insect eyes. The tyres were inflated with exposed spokes. A spare rested on the driver's side running board. Boss had the entire back seat to himself but was eager to stick his nose out of the window. Ginger opened it an inch to accommodate him.

The drive to Doncaster took over an hour on less than pristine roads. Ginger secretly wished she were behind the wheel. Basil was a very competent driver, but she was bolder and was quite sure she would've made the trip much more quickly.

Finally, they entered the town. Basil slowed to a stop next to a man strolling along the pavement. He held the hand of a young lad dressed in knickerbockers and wearing a newsboy cap. Blond tufts of hair poked out around the boy's ears, and the dark hole of a missing tooth detailed his grin. The lad reminded Ginger of her ward Scout Elliot, a young waif she'd rescued off the mean London streets and who now lived in the attic of Hartigan House with the servants.

A sharp maternal pang shot across Ginger's chest as her memories focused on Scout. Since he'd come to live with her, she hadn't been away from him for more than a day—usually, just work hours spent at her dress shop or doing benign private investigative work. Now the weeks of her honeymoon stretched before her without even a glimpse of his endearing crooked smile.

Basil asked for directions to the post office, thanked them for their time, and rounded the corner to the old building. Ginger instructed Boss to remain in the motorcar. Boss stared at her with sad brown eyes, but then curled into a ball and promptly fell asleep.

Inside the post office, the postmaster greeted the couple with a hardy "'ello."

Basil tapped his trilby and said, "I'm Chief Inspector Reed of Scotland Yard, and this is . . . La—"

Basil's gazed darted to Ginger. It was natural that they'd both, on occasion, make a slipup as they got used to her new name, but this was something different. Their operation as a detective duo worked better when it didn't appear as if the chief inspector was dragging his wife along.

Ginger finished Basil's sentence for him. "Lady Gold."

It wasn't the first time Ginger had gone by an alias in her life. Her time with the British Secret Service had given her plenty of opportunities to take on a name that wasn't her own.

"This to do wi' t'ead, then?" the postmaster said. "Ghastly business, that."

"Indeed," Basil replied.

"I don't know quite what to tell ya. Agar went about 'is business as usual. Some brute conked 'im ont' back of t'ead, emptied out t'post, and 'ung up t'bag wi' its grizzly contents inside. Agar came stumblin' back to town wi' concussion. Thankfully, that's all that ails 'im."

"Where can we find Mr. Agar?" Basil asked.

"I'm sure 'e's at 'ome restin' up." The postmaster gave them the address. "It's a cottage off t'beaten track. Tell him we're thinkin' 'bout 'im over 'ere."

Ginger linked arms with Basil as they strolled down the quaint street. "If it wasn't for the nature of our business, we could be any couple out for a leisurely stroll. So lovely to see the sun."

"That part is unexpected," Basil said. He leaned over to kiss Ginger's cheek, and she raised her chin slightly to receive it."

Back in the motorcar, Basil turned to Ginger. "I'm sorry about the name—"

"No, I think it's a good idea. When we work on a case, I should go by an alternate name. Lady Gold is as good as any."

"But only when dealing with strangers," Basil said.

"Of course," Ginger said. "Ambrosia would have my head if she thought I still laid claim to the title."

"Mrs. Reed, Lady Gold, mystery girl," Basil said. "Doesn't matter to me, so long as you are mine."

Ginger laughed. "I couldn't agree more, Mr. Reed, Chief Inspector, mystery man."

THE DRIVE to Mr. Agar's cottage was, as the postmaster had claimed, off the beaten path. Broken cobblestones with gravel patches and potholes zigzagged across the narrow road, and Ginger held onto her hat as the motorcar bounced towards Mr. Agar's house at the end of the lane. Boss, whimpering in the back, climbed over the seat and into the comfort of Ginger's lap.

"It's okay, Bossy," Ginger said. "Mr. Reed will get us there safe and sound."

Basil shot her a look, and Ginger laughed.

The little red-brick cottage was dusty with cobwebs in the corners of the windows. A similar cottage was about fifty yards closer to the main road, but other than that, the area felt rural.

"The place looks rather tired," Ginger said.

Ginger scooped Boss into her arms before following Basil to the front door. The inspector lifted the rusted knocker and let it drop. When there was no sign of movement inside he knocked more fervently. "Mr. Agar!"

"Perhaps he's sleeping?" Ginger said.

Basil knocked again, and this time they heard the shuffling of feet and the creaking of the door opening. A short, bent-over man with grey bristles growing on a fleshy face stood in the doorway. He squinted up as if the sight of them pained him.

"Whatcha want?" he asked with a strong Yorkshire accent.

"I'm Chief Inspector Reed from Scotland Yard. This is Lady Gold. Would you mind if we came in?"

The man shrugged, then winced at the pain this simple gesture caused. Ginger noted the bandage on the back of his head.

"I can't offer you no tea," he said as he carefully lowered himself into a well-worn chair. "Sorry about the mess. It's not like I got a maid or summat."

"I hope you don't mind that I have my small dog with me," Ginger said. "He's very well behaved and will stay on my lap the whole time."

"So long as you keep your distance," Mr. Agar said. "I don't like dogs."

A layer of dust covered the sparse furnishings: a wooden table with two chairs and a mismatched sofa and armchair. A stone fireplace filled one corner. A boxy radio—the most expensive item in the room—sat on the floor beside the high-backed armchair claimed by Mr. Agar. A piecrust table stood on the other side. On it was an ashtray filled with ash, several loose cigarettes, and a tarnished lighter.

Ginger and Basil took their places on the sofa, and Basil began, "Mr. Agar, can you tell us what happened yesterday?"

Mr. Agar grabbed the back of his neck. "I already tol' this to the police."

"If you wouldn't mind reciting it again," Basil said.

"Very well, it started off the same as every day. I get up early like, before the sun, especially this time of year. I go to t'office where the bag was filled from the day before. I take it to t'railway line dropping-off post. It's still pretty dark out, see, so I don't notice another bloke hiding behind these shrubs. I'm halfway up the steps to t'platform when the lights go out. Next thing I know, some copper's nudging me wi' his boot."

"You didn't see your attacker at all?" Ginger asked. "Perhaps you noticed a smell?"

Agar wrinkled his nose. "Now, that you mention it. Bloke could've used a bath."

"Are you sure about that?" Basil asked. "You just stated you didn't see or hear anyone."

"Well, no, it just came to my mind when t'lady here brought it up. I remember sniffing, thinking someone spilt summat awful on one of t'envelopes. Like sickly sweet perfume."

"Was it body odour or perfume?" Ginger asked. "Was it a lady who hit you?"

"What? No, that's norr it. You've got me all confused now. It's conk ont' head, you see. I don't remember right." Mr. Agar winced as though he was auditioning for a drama. "Now, if you don't mind, I'm feeling sick-like. Don't mean to be rude or owt."

Ginger and Basil stood at the man's dismissal.

"Thank you for your time," Basil said. "If you think of anything else, please call the police station in York and ask for me."

Basil pushed the starter button and drove the motorcar back towards York. "What did you think of Mr. Agar?" he asked.

"He seems sincerely confused," Ginger said. She kept Boss on her lap this time and scrubbed his head. "Concussion can do that. The lump under the bandage looked awful and must be painful."

"The question is still why? Why put the head in a letter bag from Doncaster?"

Good question, indeed.

CHAPTER TWENTY-ONE

Ginger let Boss out for a short walk and a chance to obey the call of nature before commanding him to get back inside the motorcar.

"Sorry, Boss. You can't come in this time."

Ginger stood beside Basil as he made his request to the nurse who greeted them at the door of the York City Nursing Home.

"I'm Chief Inspector Basil Reed from Scotland Yard."

"Oh. You must be here about Mr. Wright. Have you found him yet? I really don't understand how he got away. It's not like he could've got far. The whole staff took turns looking for him."

Ginger reached out her hand. "Hello, I'm Lady Gold. And you are?"

"Oh, forgive me. I'm Nurse Cunningham. Mr. Wright was in my charge, you see. Oh dear, do come in."

Ginger and Basil followed Nurse Cunningham—a middle-aged woman, slightly plump in the mid-section. She was dressed in the customary uniform of a nurse: all white, high-collared blouse, belted ankle-length skirt under a bibbed apron, and a white cap pinned on tied-back hair.

They settled in the staff room, and tea was offered.

"Please start from the beginning, Nurse Cunningham," Basil said. "When did you last see Mr. Wright?"

"I went to wake him up in the morning yesterday, seven a.m., as I always did. As usual, he was already awake. The elderly don't sleep for long periods of time in a row. Sore joints and things like that. I helped him bathe and dress—shave and the like—then helped him walk to the breakfast room where he ate his usual bowl of porridge and one hard-boiled egg. After that, I helped him brush his teeth and then settled him into a chair in the common room. He likes to look at the gardens and watch the birds splash in their bath. We've got three lovely stone birdbaths, you see. The patients like them."

"Is he the only patient you care for?" Ginger asked.

"Oh my, no. There's Mrs. Jones and Miss Wyatt.

They share a room and like to do everything together. Mr. Wright rises earlier, so I take care of him first."

"So, you're not watching the patients at all times," Basil said.

"That would be quite impossible. We've more patients than staff."

"When are the visiting hours?" Ginger asked.

"Normally, they're ten to four. After breakfast and before dinner. Guests are welcome to stay for lunch or can get a pass to take a resident out for short periods of time."

"Why do you say normally?" Basil asked.

"Because an exception was made, and on the day Mr. Wright went missing too."

"Oh?" Ginger prompted.

"Yes. We had an impatient and, if I may say it, impolite visitor. She caused quite a stir in the dining room. And that's when Mr. Wright went missing."

Ginger glanced at Basil. Another distraction? Similar to the one on the luggage van when the jewels were stolen?

"How long was it until you noticed Mr. Wright was gone?" Basil asked.

"I'm sorry to say at least twenty minutes. I was rather occupied."

"What did the lady look like?" Ginger asked.

"She was quite posh, I'd say, though she wasn't

dressed to match it. You can always tell by a lady's demeanour, a sense of entitlement or elitism in the eyes."

Ginger blinked at the blanket judgement. Did Nurse Cunningham see that in her as well?

As if reading the question on Ginger's face, Nurse Cunningham added quickly, "Oh, not you, my dear."

"What did she look like?"

On the taller side, slim—with well-styled hair, short with finger waves, like the youth wear it. Oh, she had a prominent mole at the corner of her lip."

"Do HURRY," Ginger said as they jumped into the motorcar. "Felicia is with Irene." As predicted earlier by Basil, both Irene Dansby and George Pierce had been released on bail.

"I'm not sure where she lives," Basil said.

Ginger dug into her handbag for the map of York she'd picked up from the police station. She laid it out on her lap and searched the index for the street name Miss Dansby had given them during their interviews. Ginger had a good memory for details like that, which was one of the qualities that had helped her tremendously during the war.

Ginger gave Basil instructions, Basil hit the accelerator without hesitation, and they hurtled down the cobbled street. Even though she was in no danger of losing it, Ginger held on to her Parisian blue-and-rose cloche hat.

Basil gave her an apologetic look. "Can't help it being bumpy, love. I'm just glad it's not the suspension of my Austin that's taking a beating."

"It's quite all right. Felicia's well-being is what's important here."

The Dansby family lived in a handsome brick terraced house in the middle of the city along the river. Ginger couldn't help but admire it, even as she raced up the pathway—Boss at her heels—to the front door. A melodious bell resounded when Ginger pushed the button and was answered by a self-important-looking butler.

"Good morning," he began.

"I'm looking for Miss Felicia Gold," Ginger said. "I believe she is with Miss Dansby."

"Indeed, she is." The butler motioned them inside. "Please wait here."

Ginger scooped Boss into her arms. The butler left them in an attractive entrance area and disappeared behind a thick wooden door.

"He's not acting as if something were amiss," Basil said. "I'm sure Felicia is quite all right."

"Of course, it's just, well, you know Felicia,"

Ginger said. "She has a way of getting herself into trouble."

The butler returned, dipped his chin, and invited Ginger and Basil to follow him. They entered a stunning sitting room with fashionable geometric wallpaper, electric chandelier, and plush furniture in the latest colours of mist-grey, jade, and powder-blue. Ginger, for all the world, couldn't imagine why someone who lived in such apparent luxury would participate in such a crime as jewel theft. Then again, the rich often had a problem with managing their funds. Or perhaps Felicia's Miss Dansby was, as she'd claimed, merely bored and was chasing a seemingly harmless thrill.

"Ginger!" Felicia said. "How is . . . everything?"

"No new news," Ginger said. Then to Irene Dansby. "Miss Dansby, how are you holding up?"

"I'm frightfully embarrassed, as you can imagine. Please Mrs. Reed, Chief Inspector, have a seat. Jones was just about to serve a light lunch. You must join us."

"You don't mind my small dog?" Ginger said. "I can put him back in the motorcar if you do."

Irene waved a well-manicured hand. "He's fine."

Basil waited for Ginger to take a seat then lowered himself in the chair closest to her. "That would be most welcome, Miss Dansby," he said. "You do understand that I must ask a few questions."

"Of course. I'll cooperate fully. I've rung my solicitor. He's on his way here from London. I'll pay restitution for my part, naturally, but I certainly will do whatever I can to stay out of prison."

"Naturally," Basil said. Ginger registered the look in his eye. The privileged elite rarely paid significantly for their crimes.

Jones, the butler, arrived with a maid in tow, and a trolley with tea and small sandwiches was rolled in. He even asked a maid to bring in a bowl of water for Boss.

Plates and teacups were filled, and the staff discreetly left the room.

"Irene was just telling me all about it," Felicia said. "A very silly thing for her to do, but she was talked into it."

"Felicia, love," Ginger said. "Please, allow the chief inspector to conduct the interview."

"And you and Mr. George Pierce are engaged to be married," Basil said. "How long has this been the status of your relationship?"

"Just before my father died."

"I'm sorry to hear that," Ginger said with sincerity. She still felt the grief of her own father's death even though he'd been gone for two years.

Irene added with a sigh, "It was his dying wish."

Ginger shot Basil a look from the corner of her eye. Such an arrangement didn't smack of romantic bliss. It would explain the tense interaction Ginger had witnessed between them.

"Was it your wish?" Ginger asked.

"I-I thought so. Now, I'm not so sure."

Basil shifted in his seat as he rested a now-empty sandwich plate on the coffee table. "Miss Dansby, was it your idea to rob Lady Pennington of her family heirloom jewels?"

Irene Dansby's delicate hands trembled slightly as she laid down her teacup and saucer.

"No. I'd never come up with such an outlandish idea on my own. I don't have a creative bone in my body, and well, this plan took some imagination."

"Was it Mr. Pierce's?" Ginger asked.

"George is less imaginative than me." Anger flashed behind dark eyes. "Really, now that I think about it, I can't believe he allowed me to get involved in such a scheme at all. He willingly let me risk my freedom, not to mention my reputation!"

"It was Mr. Burgess's idea then?" Basil said.

Irene shook her head.

"Whose idea was it?" Ginger asked.

"Like I told you before, we were gathered together by Mrs. Simms."

Felicia spat out her tea. "I knew it!"

"Knew what?" Ginger said. "You thought she was a ghost."

"I sensed *evil*," Felicia replied in her defence. "All that talk of death and robberies. Macabre!"

Basil glared at Felicia, and the younger girl shrank into her seat.

"You're saying the whole idea to rob Lady Pennington was this Mrs. Simms' alone?" Basil asked.

"Yes," Irene returned animatedly. "Brilliant, but quite off her rocker. Dresses head-to-toe in black."

"Including a widow's veil?" Ginger asked.

"Yes."

"Do you know where we can find Mrs. Simms?" Basil asked.

Irene shook her head again. "She always found us."

"She was on the train yesterday," Ginger said.

Irene's chin snapped up. "She was? How odd. I'm surprised I didn't see her."

"She entered the carriage at the opposite end from where you and Mr. Pierce were sitting," Ginger explained. The high-backed seats in first class would've blocked her view.

"Somebody must know the whereabouts of this Mrs. Simms," Basil said. "Do you know her first name?"

"I'm afraid not," Irene said.

"Where did you meet to make your plans?" Ginger asked.

"George's house. Once the three of us had agreed

to her offer, we always met there. The meetings were short, perhaps an hour or two each. Each step was her idea. George and I going to London to attend the opera, the confusion at the luggage van, it was all hers."

"What was supposed to happen to the jewels once they were in her hands?" Ginger asked.

"That's the strange thing. She didn't want them. I guess she's too old to need the money now."

"Then why?" Felicia said, butting in.

Irene Dansby shrugged. "Perhaps she didn't want Lady Pennington to have them. Perhaps she had something against the Pennington family."

Ginger was taking the last sip of her tea when Jones knocked and stepped into the sitting room. "Miss Dansby, there are two police officers at the door. They're requesting the presence of Chief Inspector Reed."

Basil jumped to his feet. "No need to get up, Miss Dansby. I'll see to them outside."

Ginger took a moment to pull Felicia aside and speak privately. "Perhaps it's time to return to London. I'm sure Ambrosia is sleeping fitfully knowing you're connected to this scandal."

"She loves a scandal!" Felicia said. "Lives for them."

"Yes, but not when her own flesh and blood is involved."

"I suppose you're right. Though I do feel bad leaving Irene alone."

"She has Mr. Pierce," Ginger said. "Actually, where is he? I'm surprised he's not here right now."

"I don't know. Irene has been glancing at the telephone all morning as if willing it to ring."

"I'm sure he'll show up. He's probably lunching with his own solicitor at the moment. I implore you to make plans to catch the late-afternoon train back to London. Will you do that?"

"If you insist. Apart from the tedious wait on the train yesterday, this has been the most excitement I've seen in donkey's years."

"Terrific. I'll come round later to take you to the station."

After saying a polite goodbye to Irene Dansby, Ginger joined Basil outside where he waited for her by the motorcar.

"Is there a problem?" she asked.

"There is for someone," he said. "A body's been found on the property belonging to George Pierce.

CHAPTER TWENTY-TWO

The Pierce house rivalled the Dansbys'. The small garden in front of the four-storey, brick and stone, terraced house was framed with a decorative iron fence. Beyond, the sun was moving lower behind a bank of fluffy clouds turning them into breathtaking rosy pinks and yellows.

Once again, Ginger had to wonder what drove a man like George Pierce, obviously in possession of considerable wealth, to do something so rash? And Miss Dansby had a point about why a man who professed to love her would be part of something like this if it relied on her involvement as well."

Basil drew the motorcar up behind the row already parked along the front kerb. He pointed through the windscreen. "Over there."

A group of officers was standing guard, one with an excited bloodhound on a leash.

"You definitely have to stay in the motorcar this time, Bossy," Ginger said. "That fellow looks like he could eat you for tea."

Wishing now that she'd worn boots rather than her black satin pumps, Ginger followed Basil to the scene at the back of the house. She never failed to ruin a pair of terrific shoes during every case, but at least this time she thought she'd be on her honeymoon, not traipsing through the damp gardens of the well-to-do.

"Looks like it was hurled over the hedge," Inspector Sullivan said. "A servant discovered it this afternoon and called the police station."

The garden was mature with thick bushes and flowerbeds. Through the damp moss and fallen leaves, Ginger could see the rear portion of a body dressed in male clothing.

"No head, I gather," Ginger said.

"Nope. Pretty much identifies the corpse unless, God forbid, there's another head lying about somewhere without its body."

"Hello!"

Ginger turned to the voice and saw the hunched-over figure of Dr. Chapman making his way towards them.

"Hello again, Dr. Chapman," she said pleasantly.

Basil and the other officers greeted the doctor with a silent nod.

Dr. Chapman set his medical bag on the ground. "What have we here?"

"Looks like the other half of Mr. Wright," Inspector Sullivan said.

Dr. Chapman knelt with one knee on the grass and took hold of one of the corpse's arms. "Male, high up in age, I'd say eighty plus."

He seemed efficient enough, but Ginger still missed Haley's straightforward, matter-of-fact approach.

The doctor continued, "Can't say what the cause of death was until I can examine the body in the lab."

Inspector Sullivan snorted. "I hope for the old chap's sake that he was dead before he lost his head."

Ginger mused: having one's head chopped off was a quick death.

"About that blood evidence we found at the exchange apparatus," Basil started, "have the results come back from the lab?"

Dr. Chapman straightened upright and brushed grass off his knees. "Yes. It belongs the victim."

"Not so surprising," Ginger said, "since we know the head was delivered from there."

Basil glanced about the building. "Where is Mr. Pierce?"

"He's inside," Inspector Sullivan said. "Mulgrew is keeping an eye on him to make sure that he doesn't make a run for it."

"You don't mind if I ask him a few questions?" Basil said.

It was a courtesy question, and Inspector Sullivan knew it. He snorted again. "Go for it."

As they circled around the house, Ginger, whilst manoeuvring carefully around the soggy soil, said to Basil, "It seems awfully convenient, don't you think?"

"Are you suggesting someone is framing Mr. Pierce?"

"It's possible."

"Or he's guilty of murder. I don't relish the idea of Felicia's feelings getting hurt by this either, but we must keep our heads."

"I'm keeping my head!" Ginger said, not appreciating the inference or the pun.

"I didn't mean to offend," Basil said. "I'm just saying we need to gather all the facts, and one of the facts is that the dead man was found in Mr. Pierce's garden."

"Of course."

Basil slowed to take Ginger's hand. "And you do have a gorgeous head."

She tapped her Parisian cloche. "It's my new hat."

. . .

George Pierce looked like he hadn't slept for a fortnight. Dark hollows circled bloodshot eyes and a shadow covered his face halfway up to his cheekbones. Ginger wagered he'd had a few too many the night before and possibly already this morning.

"Good day, Mr. Pierce," Basil said. "Do you mind if we come in?"

"I doubt I have a choice now, do I?" Mr. Pierce rudely turned on his heel and walked through the grand entrance hallway and into a doorway to another room. Ginger was afraid to speak as their voices would carry through the cavernous hall, which was sure to be double the size of the one at Hartigan House, if not more.

Without invitation, Ginger and Basil followed Mr. Pierce into what was the drawing room. Less feminine and more Victorian in flavour than the Dansby's sitting room, the Pierce drawing room was painted in deep red and had a lot of mahogany trim. Mr. Pierce sat in a high-backed leather chair in front of a raging fireplace, a crystal glass of brandy in hand.

He held it up as if giving a toast. "To the end of my youth and quite possibly my life." He emptied it back and poured himself another. "Could I interest you in a glass?"

Ginger noted the slight slur in his voice.

"It's awfully rude of me to drink whilst my guests

stand empty-handed. And by Jove, why are you still standing? You're making me nervous. Please, sit."

Ginger and Basil sat on the settee opposite Mr. Pierce.

"Drink?" he asked again.

"No, thank you," Ginger said.

Basil frowned. "A bit early for me old chap." He cleared his throat and continued. "Do you think you could answer a few questions?"

"Why not? Not much hope for me anyway now that they've found that bloody corpse in my garden. After the train fiasco, who's going to believe a word I say."

Drink was most certainly bringing out the melodrama in their suspect.

"Mr. Pierce," Basil started with authority. "Did you kill Mr. Oscar Wright?"

"I did not."

"Do you know who did?"

"I do not."

"Do you know why someone would dump his body in your garden?"

Mr. Pierce's head jerked up. "To frame me, of course."

"Why would someone want to do that?" Ginger asked.

The man shrugged. "Jealousy? Until yesterday, I

was a man to be envied. In the prime of my life, wealthy, engaged to a beautiful woman—oh, she's not going to want me now, is she? A jailbird?" He took a swig of what was left in his glass.

Well, Ginger thought, Miss Dansby was going to be a jailbird as well, but she kept that bit of trivia to herself.

"Who would be jealous enough to do that?" she asked.

"That's the thing, Mrs. Reed. I'm well liked. Respected. I admit to being stupid regarding the jewel thing, but I'd never kill anyone. Not that a jury would believe it now."

Ginger expected him to refill his glass, but instead, his chin dropped to his chest. She shared a look with Basil. Poor bloke.

"Mr. Pierce," she said gently. "Are you all right?"

Though his chin continued to sag, his eyes fluttered open. "I let my staff have the day off so I could be alone. You don't mind showing yourselves out?"

Once they were outside, Ginger said. "I think he's telling the truth. He's too drunk to be making it up."

"He admitted to the robbery," Basil said.

"But not to the murder."

"I don't know. Drunken murderers can lie to save their skin if need be."

"Yes, you're right," Ginger admitted. "But how did

he do it? And where exactly. I imagine there'd be quite a lot of blood involved in the process of decapitation. Even if the person's heart was no longer beating."

"Indeed," Basil said. "We have yet to find the initial crime scene."

They turned back to where the body was being removed, Ginger once more tiptoeing through the soft soil.

Basil stopped short and groaned.

"What is it, love?" Ginger asked, but then she saw it. Or rather, *him*. "Oh dear."

Basil let out a low growl. "Morris."

CHAPTER TWENTY-THREE

Basil shouldn't have been surprised to see his surly superintendent standing there. The severed head of a prominent national businessman was scandalous news. However, Morris' investigative technique was more like that of a bull than a bloodhound. It was well known at the Yard that the man had reached his status because of who he knew rather than what he'd accomplished on his own merits, but nothing could be done about that except hope Morris would go early into retirement.

Plus, Morris had had him thrown in jail once, and Basil hadn't forgotten that.

"Reed!" Morris bellowed. "Tell me whatcha got so far." Then, as if he had only just noticed Ginger, added, "And Mrs. Reed. A rather rough beginning to your wedding journey, eh?"

Ginger smiled back sweetly. "I love a good puzzle, Superintendent Morris. I'm happy as a clam."

Morris clucked. "You've got a fiery one, Reed, I'll give you that." He removed a cigarette case and lighter from the pocket of his trench coat and lit up. He waved the open case. "Either of you want one?"

Both Basil and Ginger shook their heads. Ginger never smoked, and though Basil liked a cigarette occasionally, Ginger refused to kiss him when he had one, so his decision not to light up was often an easy one.

"I think I'll get a lift with Dr. Chapman to Miss Dansby's place," Ginger said. "I believe I've convinced Felicia to return to London. I will accompany her to the station."

"Good idea," Basil said. "I'll meet you there."

Basil would've kissed Ginger before she left, but not in front of Morris. He watched as she chatted with the doctor and then got into his motorcar.

"From the beginning, Reed," Morris said with a tinge of impatience.

"Mrs. Reed and I were on the Flying Scotsman, boarded yesterday morning at King's Cross, when the railway security man, a Mr. Burgess, approached me to report a problem in the Royal Mail carriage. He took us to a mailbag with blood seeping out lying on the floor of the carriage. The supervisor, a Mr. Doring, showed us the contents."

"Mr. Wright's blasted head?"

"Indeed. Apparently, the postman working at the Doncaster railway mail exchange was slammed on the back of the head before he could load the bag. The mail was emptied, and a burlap bag containing the head came out."

Morris shifted his weight. "So obviously, the murder happened off the train. Looks like the chap in this grand palace had something to do with it."

"He was a passenger."

"On the Flying Scotsman?"

"Yes, sir. Along with his fiancée, Miss Irene Dansby."

"The gal your missus is on her way to?"

"Yes, sir." Basil filled him in on the botched robbery and all the main players.

"Yes, I got word of that," Morris bellowed. The superintendent had a habit of talking more loudly than circumstances required. "Would've been news had they got away with it. I'm here because of the murder."

"They may be connected," Basil said. "At least someone wants us to believe that. After all, Mr. Pierce was on the train, and now the rest of the body is found in his garden."

"I want him taken to the station. Him and that lady friend of his too."

. . .

"GINGER! I'm so glad you've come back!"

After dropping Boss off at her hotel, Ginger found Felicia alone in the Dansby's sitting room drowning in tea.

"They're coming for her."

"Who?"

"The police. Basil rang from the Pierce house to give her notice."

Ginger was warmed by Basil's thoughtfulness. He could get a good chastising if Superintendent Morris ever found out. Oh, mercy. She hoped Miss Dansby wasn't making a run for it out of the back gate.

"You don't think she has a motorcar?" Ginger asked, implying the worst.

"She wouldn't leave George. Besides, there're police about on the streets, watching."

"No sense in you staying on then?" Ginger prompted.

"I *am* rather bored. Would it be frightfully unfriendly of me to leave Irene when she's going through such a rough patch?"

"I think she's going to need a good solicitor more than a good friend. Besides, she has family, hasn't she?"

"Her mother and little sister are visiting an aunt in Bath. They've telegrammed and are on their way home."

"There you go. You can always come back once

things settle down. She'll need you more then than now, I suspect."

"Oh, Ginger, yes! Thank you. I want to go home, but I felt too guilty to suggest it."

"I'll ask the butler to ring for a taxicab."

"Will you come with me?"

"I'll go as far as the train station and see you off."

"Let me go and say goodbye to Irene. I think she'll be glad to see me go. I got the feeling she rather found me underfoot."

Not long after, a motorcar arrived at the front door of the Dansby house. The butler opened it to Constable Mulgrew.

"Hello again, Mrs. Reed," he said. "Unpleasant business we have again today."

"Indeed."

Felicia and Irene descended the stairs to the ground floor together.

"Are you sure you'll be all right?" Felicia said. Her gaze darted to the constable and back to her friend. "We could come with you, couldn't we, Ginger? It's so awful to travel in the back seat of a police motorcar alone."

"I'm afraid only Miss Dansby can come with me, Miss Gold," Constable Mulgrew said.

"We can take a taxicab to the police station, then," Felicia insisted.

"Felicia, darling," Irene said with a sigh. "As you've said, it's just routine questioning. I'll be fine. My solicitor is meeting me there. I'm just sorry that you got mixed up in all of this. It's dreadfully embarrassing. Not at all how I imagined entertaining you during your visit."

"Once things have settled, I'll come again. Or if you're in London—"

"Miss Dansby?" Constable Mulgrew said. "We need to go."

"Very well." Irene made a show of giving Felicia a tight embrace, and Ginger felt pity for the two friends. Felicia's large eyes filled with tears.

"Now, now," Ginger said gently. "You don't want to miss the train. The taxicab awaits us."

GINGER HELD her white-gloved hand in the air and waved Felicia off as the train chugged out of the station, and when she turned, she nearly bumped into Basil.

"Oh mercy, Basil, you startled me."

"So sorry, my dear." He took her by the arm and guided her through the station. "I met Mulgrew at the police station. He said you'd be here."

"Thank you for coming for me."

"Always my pleasure," Basil said. Ginger felt her

cheeks grow rosy at her new husband's obvious affection, despite a very British effort to hold in his emotions.

"So where to now?" Ginger asked. "The Wright house?"

"My thoughts exactly," Basil said.

They reached their borrowed motorcar, and Basil held the passenger door open for her. Once behind the wheel, he asked, "How's Felicia?"

Ginger tipped the rearview mirror her way and checked her reflection. Hat straight, the makeup highlighting green eyes unsmudged. Her lipstick could use another application, but she'd wait until she was alone to do that. She adjusted the tips of her red bob to reinforce the curls that rested against each cheek and swung the rearview mirror back.

Basil smirked as he corrected the position for his perspective. "Are we ready?"

Ginger smirked back. "Of course."

"It was Superintendent Morris' idea to take Mr. Pierce and Miss Dansby into the police station for questioning. I hope she wasn't too distressed," Basil said.

"She's quite distraught about George," Ginger said. "I hope she's not implicated in any way herself."

"If they have anything on Pierce, they could very well arrest her for accessory. Even if she wasn't involved in any way. If they can show she knew something and didn't report it, she'd be an accessory after the fact.

Ginger sighed. It was a terrible situation for Irene Dansby but also a heartbreak for poor Felicia.

Unlike either the Dansby or Pierce homes, the Wright house was smack in the middle of the city behind York Minster: a massive Gothic Cathedral with vast stained-glass windows. It was an impressive three-storey brick house with a small but well-tended-to garden. A black wreath hung on the tall wooden door of the dead man's home.

Ginger eyed it soberly. "Sometimes I get so caught up in the puzzle of the crime, I forget about the grief suffered in its wake."

"Indeed," Basil said. "There's only a son, I'm told. Mrs. Wright passed away nearly twenty years ago."

Their knock on the door was answered by a diminutive, timid-looking maid. "Mr. Ronald Wright isn't taking visitors, I'm afraid. You understand, I'm sure."

"I'm afraid this isn't a sympathy visit." Basil explained the reason for their call.

"Oh dear. Very well, come in."

The maid disappeared. The house was well-kept, if outdated. In need of a woman's touch, Ginger mused.

"By first appearances, I shouldn't think Mr. Wright

was killed for money's sake," Basil said. "One would expect a millionaire tycoon to live rather extravagantly.

Ginger concurred. "Perhaps he was miserly, hording his riches."

"Or lost his fortune somehow. I'll ask Sullivan for an update on Mr. Wright's financial affairs."

The maid returned. "Please follow me."

The Wright drawing room was very masculine with straight lines, dark wood, and not a floral likeness —real or in the design—to be seen. Mr. Ronald Wright, a man in his fifties with thinning salt-and-pepper hair cut short, and a matching moustache, rose to his feet. Politely, he shook hands.

"I'm Chief Inspector Reed," Basil said. "And this is my wife, Mrs. Reed. Our condolences on the loss of your father."

"Thank you. How may I help you?" Mr. Wright Junior had a suitable air of mourning—loose shoulders and sagging mouth—but something in his eyes made Ginger think that the man wasn't quite so sorry his father was gone than he'd like people to believe.

"I'd like to ask a few questions," Basil said. "Just a matter of form."

Ginger and Basil had barely been seated on the dark leather settee when the maid returned with a tea tray.

"That was fast," Ginger said.

The maid responded quietly. "I asked the cook to put the kettle on as soon as you arrived, madam."

The tea was poured, blown upon, and sipped carefully. Then Basil jumped right in.

"When was the last time you saw your father alive?"

"At the weekend. I always visit him at the weekend."

"How long has he been a resident at the nursing home?"

"Coming up to two years now."

"Did you father have enemies?"

Ronald Wright took a long sip of his tea. His clear blue eyes scanned the room as if he were deep in thought and trying to dredge up an answer. Ginger had the feeling there were plenty of enemies, and that Mr. Wright Junior was about to lie or make light of them.

"Well, anyone in that level of management is bound to have dissenters. As owner of the largest textile mill in Yorkshire, my father made a few unpopular decisions. I suppose a loony might've gone off his rocker at some insignificant thing he didn't happen to agree with. I mean, it's clearly a loony, isn't it? Who else would kill a man in such a ghastly fashion?"

"Do you have any enemies, Mr. Wright?" Ginger asked.

Ronald Wright appeared stunned by the insinuation.

"I highly doubt someone would try to get to me by cutting off my father's head, *Mrs. Reed.*"

She most definitely needed to stick with Lady Gold. Rightly or wrongly, the title itself carried a lot of weight, and Ginger didn't think Mr. Wright would be so rude and condescending to a *Lady*.

"My wife has a point," Basil said, and Ginger smiled at him appreciatively. "Indeed, it is not out of the realm of possibility that a person, a loony if you prefer, might lash out at you by attacking your father. I see it quite often in my line of work, the concept that a person can hurt their foe more deeply by hurting someone they love."

"Yes, very well," Ronald consented in a huff. "I have my share of 'enemies' if you like. Associates who are unhappy with how I've conducted myself in business, but hardly a reason to kill my father. Besides, people who know me well enough to want to hurt me, realise I wasn't close to my father.

"Does your father still have a bedroom here?" Ginger asked. "Are his personal items in the house?"

Ronald replied slowly, "Yes."

"Would you mind if we had a look?" Basil asked. "There could be a clue among his things that might lead us to a suspect."

"I suppose so. Just don't shift things around. The housekeeper won't like it."

Ronald Wright led them to a room at the back of the house. "This used to be his study, but once the steps got to be too much for him, we set his bedroom up here. Never bothered to set it back."

The interior of the house didn't portray great wealth. Perhaps Mr. Wright had indeed made a few bad investments, or possibly, he was simply frugal by nature. Tall windows overlooked the back garden and, Ginger thought, would shed a nice amount of natural light during the daytime. Now that darkness had fallen, they were left to the overhead electric light fixture, which cast dim shadows. A single mattress was pressed up against a wall beside a simple bedside table with a gas lamp, unlit. A wardrobe had one door jutting open.

"It doesn't close properly," Ronald said. "Loose latch. Never bothered to get it fixed."

Ronald lingered near the door, not trusting them to be left alone. Ginger wondered what he was afraid they'd find.

Ginger opened the wayward door, expecting to find an assortment of men's suits, perhaps a couple of pairs of leather shoes but instead, the only thing occupying the cupboard was an old-fashioned, heavy-looking safe, the kind locked with a key.

Basil stood behind her and peered over her shoulder. "How interesting." He spun around to face Ronald Wright. "Do you have a key to the safe?"

Ronald shook his head. "Father never discussed his private affairs with me."

"Who do you think would have a key?" Ginger asked.

"His solicitor, I suspect. He's as old as the hills too. I'll give him a ring, and hopefully, we can get it from him before he knocks off."

"Please ring the police station once you have it," Basil asked. "I'll get an officer to come to the house to keep an eye on Mr. Wright's room."

"You don't trust me not to open it, eh?"

Basil stared him down. "No offence, Mr. Wright, but this is a murder investigation, and certain procedures must be followed. Now, if you don't mind, I'd like to use your telephone."

CHAPTER TWENTY-FOUR

Ginger and Basil waited for Constable Mulgrew to arrive before leaving Ronald Wright alone with his father's safe.

"Do you suppose Dr. Chapman might have some news by now?" Ginger said as she slipped into the motorcar."

"Let's head to the mortuary and find out?"

The streets of York weren't designed for motor vehicle traffic, and often, they had to pull over against the flat brick façade of terraced houses to make way for another motorcar to pass.

"Do you think Ronald Wright might've killed his father?" Basil said after one particularly tight manoeuvre. "A crime of passion such as this is often committed by close relations."

Ginger nodded. "If this was the wife, the husband would be the prime suspect."

"Exactly."

"Speaking of wives, have you noticed the response we're getting from people when you introduce me as your wife?" Ginger said. "I'm not being taken seriously, and neither are you for that matter?"

"I have noticed. Shall we carry on with your Lady Gold persona?"

"People seem to be more agreeable to that. I should continue to operate my private investigative business under that name. In fact, my cards say it—Lady Gold. Private Investigator. You wouldn't mind, love, would you? I know we've mentioned it before in jest, but I'm asking seriously now. It wouldn't be too misleading?"

"I think it's an acceptable plan. I'll call you my associate from Lady Gold's private investigative agency. And if people learn that you're also my wife, so be it."

"Thank you, darling," Ginger said with relief. "It's rather late, in some regards, to begin with that on this case, but the next one."

Basil laughed. "You're already on the next one? Let's solve this one first, shall we?"

Dr. Chapman greeted them at the hospital

mortuary and led them to the body draped discreetly under a sheet on a white ceramic table. The head was on a second one, also covered.

"What have you discovered, Dr. Chapman?" Basil asked.

Dr. Chapman lowered the sheet. Ginger couldn't help grimace at the grizzly stub of the man's neck with severed veins, torn muscle and sinew, and chiselled bone exposed. Dr. Chapman lifted one shoulder to reveal the bluish-white flesh of the back. A single wound was apparent under the left shoulder blade.

"Knife wound?" Ginger said.

Dr. Chapman lowered the shoulder of the corpse down. "Indeed. This is what killed him. A direct stab to the heart. It explains the shortage of blood from the severed head. There was no pulse when the axe dropped. The victim was already dead."

"This is very perplexing," Ginger said. "Why not just leave the man's body alone once the deed was done? Why the big show with the head on the train?"

"My thoughts exactly," Basil said. "This is more than simple revenge. It was a message to someone on the train."

"Yes, but who?" Ginger said. "Irene and George? Mr. Burgess or Mr. Doring? The other first-class passengers?"

"That's what we need to find out."

CHAPTER TWENTY-FIVE

The evening meal was much overdue, and Ginger suggested they went back to the hotel before heading out. She wanted to change into a more suitable dress and reapply her makeup. Basil reclined on the bed, content to watch her.

"Might it be a message for Lady Pennington?" Ginger asked as she ran a brush through her hair.

"So far we've not been able to find any connection between the Pennington family in Edinburgh and the Wrights of York. They've met socially, but not often, and nothing incriminating."

"It's so curious how Lady Pennington's jewels and the plan to steal them happened on the same train as the delivery of Mr. Wright's head."

"A Venn diagram of the robbery and the murder would find Miss Dansby and Mr. Pierce in the overlapping section, I'm afraid," Basil said. "They were also at Lady Pennington's opera."

Ginger sighed. "So true. But we mustn't forget Mr. Burgess and Mr. Carney. They were involved in the attempted robbery."

"As was Miss Dansby and Mr. Pierce. I'm sorry, love, but it doesn't look good for Felicia's friends."

"Even if they did stab Mr. Oscar Wright, I just can't imagine either one chopping off the man's head. And even if they did—which, as I've said, I just can't imagine—they were on the train when the head was deposited. They couldn't have knocked Mr. Agar out and swapped the mailbags."

"There must be an accomplice then."

"Who?"

Basil worked his lips and rubbed his chin. "Mr. Ronald Wright, perhaps?"

"Oh, mercy." Ginger said. Then changing the subject completely, she spun around displaying a silver lamé evening dress by Murielle's of Glasgow. It had thin straps with a deep plunging backline, fine gold embroidery design and a wide gold hem that landed mid-shin. She wore a black brimless hat that allowed just a frame of red hair over her forehead and curled along her cheeks. A long strand of silver pearls and black T-strap sandals finished the outfit. She twirled for Basil's benefit. "What do you think?"

Basil swung his legs off the bed and bolted to his feet. "I think we'd better leave right this moment, or I might pull you to this bed and miss out on dinner all together."

Ginger laughed. "Clearly, it's much too dangerous for us to stay in this room."

Boss barked as if he agreed.

They decided on the ease and convenience of the hotel restaurant and took the same table they'd sat at the night before.

"Look," Ginger said. "We're not the only ones to return. There's Mr. Doring. And the Fishers."

"No Mr. Burgess or Mrs. Griffiths?"

"I suppose we can't be as lucky as that. Do you have more questions for any of them?"

"I'm sure something will come to me."

They ordered their meals along with a bottle of chardonnay.

"I'm going to use the ladies," Ginger said. "And stop to say hello to the Fishers on my way."

"Good idea," Basil said. "I might do the same and have a chat with Mr. Doring at the bar."

"Hello, Mr. Fisher and Mrs. Fisher," Ginger said with a big smile.

"Good day, Mrs. Reed," Mr. Fisher said.

"I'm surprised to see you haven't left York." Ginger couldn't think of a reason Inspector Sullivan would require them to stay another day. "Surely the police have said you're free to go?"

"Oh yes. But York is so lovely, isn't?" Mrs. Fisher said. "We decided to spend a few days here now, rather than go all the way to Scotland."

And perhaps, stay to watch the drama they started unfold?

"We didn't want to spend this rather nice day on the train," Mr. Fisher added. "And who knows if tomorrow will be as pleasant."

"So true," Ginger agreed. "The British weather is very unpredictable."

"And you?" Mrs. Fisher said. "You're staying on?" There was another question underlying that one—*how's the case going?*

"Just for a little while longer," Ginger answered, keeping her expression neutral. She had no intention of giving anything away. "By the way, I was wondering if you've seen Mrs. Griffiths?"

"I imagine she's gone home," Mrs. Fisher said, her nose jutting into the air. "I believe she lives in the area. Strange one, isn't she? I don't mean to gossip, but that lady has been alone too long, if you know what I mean."

"I'm sure I don't," Ginger replied.

Mrs. Fisher was unruffled. "A busybody, is what I'm saying." She tilted her head and stared up at

Ginger. "Well, I'm certain you've formed your own opinions about us, haven't you Mrs. Reed?"

Ginger smiled. "I hope you enjoy the rest of your time here."

"And you too, Mrs. Reed."

Basil was already at their table when Ginger returned, and their food had arrived.

"What do the Fishers know?" Basil asked as he cut into his steak and kidney pie.

"They've decided to holiday in York instead of Edinburgh, though I think they're curious to witness the outcome of this case."

Basil raised a dark brow. "A little too curious?"

"Either one of them could've masqueraded as Mrs. Simms," Ginger said. "And when I questioned her about Mrs. Simms, she mentioned how we were all going to be like her one day—old and in mourning. Perhaps she was having a hard time keeping her own secret."

"You think she was referring to herself as Mrs. Simms?"

"It's possible."

Ginger took a bite of her poached halibut in lemon sauce, and let out a soft hum of approval. "I asked what they knew about Mrs. Griffiths. All they know is that she lives around here."

"The address she reported doesn't exist."

"It's possible that someone wrote it down wrong."

"Or she's purposely misleading us." Basil sipped his wine. "Unfortunately, Sullivan didn't have anything to hold her with, and it's not a crime to make a mistake on your address."

"She's an odd fish, isn't she?" Ginger said.

"Plenty of those type around."

"What about Mr. Doring?"

"He's taken sick leave, though I'm not certain Scotch counts as a medicinal concoction."

Ginger sympathised. "Some people can't cope with the sight of blood and gore. And this death was particularly gruesome."

"Indeed. Though I can't help but wonder if Mr. Doring's poor disposition is perhaps due to a guilty conscience."

THE NEXT DAY Ginger and Basil drove to the scene of the crime. Two officers were posted at the sidelined carriages. Basil showed his police identification.

"We're going to have a walk along the tracks," he said.

Ginger, bundled in her fur-trimmed wool coat and matching hat, braced against the chilly breeze. At least the sun poked out from behind the clouds every so often for a flash of warmth. She led Boss along on his leash.

After a half-hour walk, they had found nothing but bits of litter tucked in along the tracks and a stray cat meowing at being disturbed.

"If our Mrs. Simms tossed her cane out of the window," Ginger said, as she scoured the ground, "she would've done it closer to London than York. She went missing whilst we were dining."

"I thought of that too," Basil said. "Sullivan's got the railway police on the lookout."

WITH NO LUCK at the crime scene, they headed back to Doncaster. When they reached the road near the railway exchange where the bag swap occurred, Basil pulled over, parked, and a new search for evidence began. Ginger was afraid they were going to, once again, end up with nothing, when Boss started to sniff the dirt with urgency.

"What is it, Bossy?"

Boss whined then sat back on his haunches. He wasn't about to move until Ginger discovered what he'd found. She bent down and saw this spot was a mite darker than the rest. "Basil, I think we have blood."

Basil knelt, carefully gathered a small patch of

stained gravel, and put it in an evidence bag. "I'll get Dr. Chapman to confirm whether it matches our victim's. I'm surprised the officers who patrolled this area didn't see it."

"The weather was nasty. It wouldn't have stood out like it does now that the ground has dried. Besides, it was Boss's discovery. We wouldn't have seen it otherwise."

"It's a wonder the blood didn't wash away."

"Perhaps there was more that did." Ginger climbed the steps to the podium. "There are a couple of spots on the wood here too, where the bag would've been hanging."

"Strange, that," Basil said. "I would think the post bags would have been sealed in case of bad weather or other eventualities."

"Yes, and Dr. Chapman said that Mr. Wright had been killed before his head was removed, and therefore, there wasn't a lot of blood."

Basil gave her a look of interest. "The killer's blood, then?"

"Perhaps he cut himself on something." Ginger searched for a nail or protruding object that might've caused the injury but found nothing.

"I'll have to get samples from Mr. Pierce and Miss Dansby," Basil said.

Ginger sighed. "I suppose you must."

"It might not be a match, which would be evidence in their favour."

"One can only hope." Ginger said. *But if the sample didn't belong to one of them, whose blood was it?*"

Further investigation found nothing and a repeat of their performance along the tracks in York garnered the same.

"We still don't know how Mrs. Simms—whoever she, or he, might be—vanished into thin air," Ginger said. "I can only conclude that the person we met was in disguise, which would explain the cane tip. But where did the rest of the costume go? And who was wearing it?"

"This is a bizarre case, indeed," Basil said with a shake of his head.

"Do you think Mr. Wright's lawyer might've shown up with the safe key?" Ginger asked.

"Let's go to the police station and find out."

CHAPTER TWENTY-SIX

Constable Mulgrew confirmed that the Wright family solicitor was on his way and if they left soon, Ginger and Basil would likely arrive just as he did.

Basil was getting his bearings in York, and the drive to Mr. Wright's house was easy to navigate. He reached for Ginger's hand and kissed it.

"I like us working together like this," he said.

"You just like keeping an eye on me," Ginger teased. "Admit it."

"Well, that part is true."

Basil had confessed his concern and worry about Ginger and the dangerous situations her private detective work got her into. He wished she would stop. He didn't mind that she worked. She had her dress shop to keep her occupied. The problem was his new wife was too intelligent—and too experienced—to be satisfied with a more traditional role.

He knew this about her when he let himself fall in love. He knew this about her when he asked her to marry him. He knew he'd signed up for a lifetime of concern for his curious and courageous wife.

It was unconventional for an officer of the law to consult his wife, but Ginger, before they were married, had proved to be invaluable. Her intuition, her eye for detail, indeed, all the covert skills she'd acquired through her mysterious work in the Great War had proved beneficial. She had a natural way with people—they put down their guard and opened up rather than clamming up like they did when he did the interviews on his own.

Ginger squeezed his hand back. "I like keeping an eye on you too."

"Then it's a beneficial situation for both of us."

Constable Mulgrew's prediction was correct. Just as they pulled up, the solicitor arrived in a flashy motorcar—pale green with gold-plated chrome.

Basil whistled his approval. "That Morris Oxford is a beaut. This bloke doesn't work for nothing that's for sure."

As they all approached the front entrance, Basil made introductions. "I'm Chief Inspector Reed of

Scotland Yard. I'm in charge of this case. This is my associate, Lady Gold."

Basil grinned in Ginger's direction, and she held on to a smile that threatened to break out.

"I'm Mr. Briggs. Mr. Oscar Wright's solicitor." The man was angular with deep-set hooded eyes, one of which held tightly to a monocle. "I understand you wish to get into my client's safe."

"That is correct," Basil said.

The door was answered by Ronald Wright himself. A cigarette hung from the corner of his mouth, and Ginger wondered if he would let the long ash fall to the parquet flooring.

"Jolly good," he said. "I'm dying to get to the bottom of this."

A standing ashtray inside the study received the ashes just in time. With another billow of smoke, Mr. Wright said, "There's an inquest, of course. Just got a telephone call. Tomorrow, two o'clock."

Ginger made a mental note. Their honeymoon would be postponed for a few more days yet.

"Shall we get to it?" Mr. Briggs said.

Ronald Wright made a show of opening the wardrobe doors and revealing the safe. Mr. Briggs removed a key from his pocket and put it in the lock. It felt as if everyone was holding their breath as the solicitor turned the key.

Click.

"I'll remove the items," Mr. Briggs said, "and lay them on the table. I'll be itemising them for the record.

"Oh Lord," he said when he looked inside. Mr. Briggs' eyes widened, and his monocle dropped from its position and dangled from the string around his neck.

Ronald Wright wasn't patient enough to wait for his solicitor to remove whatever was inside. He elbowed his way in, nearly knocking Ginger over. His mouth gaped.

Basil, huffing with impatience, stepped in front of the safe, allowing Ginger room to peer inside.

"Oh mercy," she said. Along with a few legal papers were several bars of gold.

CHAPTER TWENTY-SEVEN

"Well, I'll be damned!" Ronald said. "He always told me the company profits had to go back into the company. I've lived beneath my peers whilst Father was sitting on twenty bars of gold?"

"It's quite likely these are stolen, Mr. Wright," Basil said, staring hard at the man. "Are you certain you knew nothing about them?"

"I swear on my mother's grave. Father never talked about his past. Water under the bridge, he'd say."

Basil faced the solicitor. "What about you, Mr. Briggs? Were you aware of the contents of Mr. Wright's safe?"

"Certainly not. In fact, he was very tight-lipped, which I found rather annoying, to be honest. His instructions were very clear that no one was to open the safe except with his consent and in his presence. Of course, now that he has passed away, his verbal request is no longer binding."

Ginger stared at Ronald.

"Don't look at me," he said, flashing his palms. "Father confided in me least of all. Lord knows where he's hidden his copy of the key. I certainly don't."

Ginger mused: Does the son of the dead man protest too much?

Standing on the tips of her glossy red, gold-embossed, Russian-influenced shoes by Gronberg, Ginger stared over Mr. Briggs' slumped shoulders. "Are those official change of name papers?"

Basil nudged his way in and picked the documents up. "It appears that Oscar Wright was born with the name Simon Fowler."

"That's odd," Ginger said. "Why would he change his name?"

Basil turned to the son who looked sincerely baffled. "Let me see those!"

Basil handed the document to the solicitor who gave them to Ronald. The younger man shook his head. "I had no idea, and I've got no idea as to why."

"I think I have," Basil said. His eyes darted to the gold bars. "Simon Fowler was part of the group involved in The Great Gold Robbery of 1855."

"That robbery, again?" Ginger mused aloud.

Ronald Wright sniggered, his eyes bright with hilarity. "Are you serious, old chap? My father, a train robber? Had I known that I might've actually respected the man!"

"Crime is not to be respected," Basil said.

Ronald had the sense to look sheepish. "Well, no, I just meant he had gumption, that's all."

"Mr. Briggs," Basil said. "Kindly lock the items in the safe and then give me the key. Mr. Wright, the police will stay on site until the contents can be collected. Please don't leave town."

Once they were in the motorcar and driving back to the police station, Ginger said, "Mr. Ronald Wright's shock seemed sincere. It amazes me the kind of secrets that are kept in families."

"Indeed." Basil adjusted the rearview mirror. A horse and carriage pulled in behind him. "It brings up the question: does this gold have something to do with Wright's demise?"

BASIL AND GINGER had returned to the police station hoping to interview Miss Dansby, Pierce and Burgess again. Basil excused himself briefly to make enquiries and when he returned he said, "Apparently our suspects have called on their solicitors and refuse to see us."

Ginger pouted in that way that made Basil's pulse beat a little faster. If it weren't for this blasted case—

"What about Mr. Burgess?"

Basil removed his trilby and returned it, forcing himself to get his mind back on task. "I think he wants to make a deal."

"Hopefully that desire will make him eager to talk," Ginger said.

As they waited for the interview to be arranged, Inspector Sullivan called out. "Chief Inspector! I've got news on your cane."

"What is it?" Basil asked.

"The railway police found a black cane discarded by the tracks near Huntingdon. It's on its way to the lab here in York. I'll let you know once the fingerprinting has been done." Sullivan grinned like the cat who had eaten the canary. "I've got more good news. Burgess has agreed to see you."

Mr. Burgess' Adam's apple appeared to climb and descend an invisible ladder. Ginger thought he *looked* like a guilty man. She also knew from experience that looks could be deceiving.

Basil seemed to notice the man's nerves too. "Do you need a glass of water?" he asked.

Mr. Burgess cleared his throat. "If you don't mind."

Basil nodded to the officer standing guard by the door. He returned shortly with a cup of water and gave it to the suspect.

"You know you have a right to have a solicitor present," Basil said.

"I can't afford no solicitor," Burgess spat, disregarding the admonition.

Basil flipped to a new page in his notebook. "The courts will assign you one."

Burgess shook his head belligerently. "I was framed. No solicitor can prove that. I need the likes of you to help me."

"What makes you believe you were framed, Mr. Burgess?" Ginger asked.

"Ain't it obvious? I'm sitting here, ain't I? I didn't kill no one."

Unflustered by Mr. Burgess' outburst, Ginger continued, "But you conspired to steal the Pennington jewels."

Burgess shrugged. "Sure, I'll put my hand up to that one, but it ain't no murder. Those posh nobs have enough money, it wasn't like they'd miss a beat in their good life, once a day of bemoaning their *bad fortune* had passed." He made a face. "There's some who need it more."

"Like you?"

Mr. Burgess shrugged again. "I'd like to retire."

"We're gathering evidence that could convict you of murder," Basil said. Ginger knew it was a bluff—they had nothing close to it—but Mr. Burgess didn't know that.

"Like I said, I'm being framed."

"By whom?" Basil asked.

Mr. Burgess laughed dryly. "Some old biddy, that's who. Shows up at my door one day, says she has an offer I can't refuse."

Ginger leaned in. "A Mrs. Simms?"

"That's right. Completely batty if you ask me."

Basil shared a quick look with Ginger before saying, "She came to your house?"

"That's right."

"How did she know where you live?" Ginger asked

"She knew a lot of stuff about us that she shouldn't know."

Basil scribbled something down, then asked, "Is she blackmailing you?"

"Well, sort of."

Tapping the tip of his pencil on the table, Basil said, "It's rather hard to be *sort of* blackmailed, Mr. Burgess. Either you are or your aren't."

Mr. Burgess patted his forehead with a well-used handkerchief. "It's like this. She comes to my door, asks to speak privately. Says she knew my father. Has something on him and thinks she can implicate me. She even asked if I had his blood in me. I asked her what she meant by that. Course I have my own dad's blood in me. I ain't adopted."

"Who's your father?" Basil asked.

"James Burgess. He was a railway guard, like me."

The name sounded familiar. Basil frowned as he tried to recollect why.

"Ha! You're trying to remember, aren't you? My dad was tried for train robbery," Burgess offered.

Basil's eyes widened as the facts clicked in. "The Great Gold Robbery?"

Basil gave Ginger a meaningful glance. *This is the robbery Mrs. Simms' had referred to on the Flying Scotsman*, he thought.

"That's right," Mr. Burgess said glibly. "He served his time. Got quite a beating whilst in prison. Couldn't work when they let him out. Me and my brother got saddled with taking care of him and my mother.

"Why would the railway give you a job?" Ginger asked.

"Why not? It weren't me that robbed the train in '55. I was just a little 'un. But come to think of it, I think good ol' Dad did grease some palms to get me in if you know what I mean."

"So, Mrs. Simms appeared out of the blue and offered you a chance to steal the Pennington jewels," Basil stated.

"That's right."

Basil grinned as if he were impressed. "The Great Train Robbery of '24?"

"Could've been, I suppose," Mr. Burgess returned smugly. "Would've made the papers anyway."

Basil continued to press. "You would've liked that."

"Sure, but it ain't like my name would've been in them. We weren't supposed to get caught. We met at Pierce's place at least a dozen times to go through every detail."

"Why *did* you get caught, Mr. Burgess?" Ginger asked.

"You know why? That damn head."

Ginger seemed unperturbed by the swearing. Basil knew she'd heard far worse in the war. "And you didn't kill Mr. Wright."

"I did not. I was on the train."

"Mr. Wright was killed the night before."

"Oh, well."

Basil leaned back and looked Mr. Burgess in the eye. "Where were you two nights ago from dusk to dawn?"

Mr. Burgess laughed. "Sleeping like honest folk do."

"Are you sure about that?" Ginger asked.

"I wasn't in no shed chopping off a man's head."

Basil narrowed his gaze. "Who said Mr. Wright was killed in a shed."

"Just a guess, sir," Mr. Burgess said quickly. "Just a guess."

CHAPTER TWENTY-EIGHT

Ginger and Basil returned to their hotel room to prepare for the inquest. Boss lay on the bed as Basil waited on the pincushion chair. Ginger sat at the dressing table mirror applying her makeup. "The train robbery of 1855," she began as she added dusky shadow to her eyelid, "was before my time, of course, but I'd heard about it, naturally. There are plenty of train robberies in America as well." Ginger's mind flashed to her childhood home in Boston. "Father shipped steel via the railways and was a victim once himself."

"Mrs. Simms brought up the train robbery of '55 when she first entered our compartment," Basil said. "I'm beginning to think that wasn't happenstance."

"I agree, darling," Ginger said. "She was playing with us. It was her first move."

"And now we find that the victim was one of the robbers," Basil said.

"Don't forget Mr. Burgess." Ginger kissed a handkerchief to seal her lipstick. "His father was also involved in the robbery, and Mrs. Simms targeted him specifically."

Boss' head shot up at the sound of a knock on the door. Basil answered it.

"A message for Mrs. Reed." The porter handed Basil a folded piece of paper. Basil tipped him and closed the door.

"What does it say?" Ginger asked.

"Miss Dansby has made a specific request to speak to you. Apparently, she'll talk to no one else."

"Oh, but if I go now, I'll miss the inquest."

"I can safely predict the coroner is going to conclude 'murder by a person or persons unknown.'"

"You're right," Ginger said. "I'm dying to hear what Miss Dansby has to say."

Basil pulled Ginger in for a quick kiss. "Don't get your lipstick on me, love," he said with a smile. "It's not professional."

The inquest began half an hour before Ginger's appointment to see Irene, so Basil took a taxicab and left Ginger the motorcar. A minor altercation with another driver (and a slight scratch on the bumper) delayed her arrival at the Crown Court. After taking a moment to collect herself, she hurried inside and announced her arrival to the clerk. A middle-aged officer with a slight limp escorted her across the circular lawn to the female prison. A few minutes later, he directed her to an interview room where Irene Dansby was waiting.

Ginger took the lone empty chair. "Miss Dansby, how are you holding up?"

Irene Dansby, dressed simply in a cotton day frock and without makeup, looked like a forlorn little girl who'd lost her mother. Her bottom lip quivered, and Ginger hoped she wasn't about to burst into tears. The girl had bitten off more than she could chew.

"As well as to be expected. I didn't sleep much last night. I know I look frightful."

Irene's appearance was the least of Miss Dansby's problems, but Ginger commiserated.

"It's all terribly trying, I know."

"It's a living nightmare, that's what it is, Mrs. Reed. I only wanted a bit of adventure, and to please—"

Ginger finished the sentence for her. "Mr. Pierce?"

"Oh dear. I don't want to get him into trouble."

Ginger fancied Mr. Pierce had got himself into trouble. She changed tactics. "What happened at the York City Nursing Home, Miss Dansby?"

Irene Dansby blinked hard, apparently losing her tongue.

"Miss Dansby?" Ginger prompted.

"It was Mrs. Simms! She asked me to go to the nursing home on Monday, create a scene, and leave after fifteen minutes." She looked up from under damp eyelashes. "I was to demand to see an old uncle, completely fabricated, and proceeded to have a fit when they couldn't produce him. Then I was to 'recall' that I had the wrong home."

"Did Mrs. Simms say why she wanted you to create a diversion?" Ginger asked.

Irene shook her head causing short curls to bounce around her jawline. "I didn't ask."

"Why not?"

Irene's eyes silently pleaded as they landed on Ginger.

"Are you being blackmailed?" Ginger asked.

Irene's bottom lip started trembling again, and this time, a tear travelled slowly down one cheek. "Somehow she found out about a . . . moment of impropriety on my part, and said she'd tell George if I didn't do this for her. I swear, I had nothing to do with Mr. Wright's death."

"But you did, didn't you," Ginger said gently. "Mr. Wright was taken from the home unnoticed because of the part you played."

Ginger could see the window of cooperation close as Irene stiffened. "I have no more to say to you, Mrs. Reed. Guard!"

WITH TIME TO spare before the inquest was due to end, Ginger asked directions to the York Library. The key to this mystery was this "Mrs. Simms." They had to discover her true identity. The librarian showed her to the archives section where Ginger asked to look for information on English families with the surname Simms.

As they said, back in Boston, Simms were a dime a dozen.

Ginger knew nothing about Mrs. Simms—her age, her first name, her address, or even if she'd ever been married. Perhaps she was like Mrs. Beasley, Ginger's cook at Hartigan House, and the title of Mrs. was a courtesy.

Perhaps she wasn't even a *she*.

What *did* she know about this mystery person? She used a cane. Did she need it, or was it a ruse? No, she didn't need it. She'd tossed it out of the lavatory window and continued on without it. She liked the morbid and sensational. She'd immediately talked about the hanging of Susan Newell, and that famous train robbery.

Ginger inclined her head in thought. That train robbery had had a way of coming up over the last few days. She asked the librarian for newspapers for 1855 and particularly 15 May and onwards.

All the headlines were similar. GREAT GOLD ROBBERY. Ginger read from the London Morning Post, Wednesday, 16 May 1855.

Two hundred pounds of gold en route to Paris worth £12,000 has been stolen. Three London firms each sent a box of gold bars and coins from London Bridge station to Paris via the South Eastern Railway. This audacious crime was discovered when the boxes were opened and it was found that they were all full of lead shot. No further details have been submitted by the police to the press, however, it is easily established that this is the first train robbery to take place in England.

The rest of the week's stories gave few details, only that the enquiries by the Metropolitan Police, the South Eastern Railway Police, and the French Police Forces, were extensive. It'd come to light that when the boxes of "gold" had arrived by boat in Boulogne, France, one had weighed forty pounds less than it should've done. However, for some reason this discrepancy wasn't taken seriously and the boxes were transported the rest of the way to Paris by rail.

South Eastern Railway offered a reward. For

several months the papers reported a suspicion the crime had occurred in France.

A familiar name jumped off the page.

The latest suspect in what is now universally known as The Great Gold Robbery is one James Burgess. For thirteen years, Burgess has worked in railway service, and it has come to light he was working on the South Eastern Railways line on the night in question. However, after questioning, the police have stated that nothing new has been established, and Mr. Burgess was released.

James Burgess Sr., Ginger thought, was to be found guilty. Who else was involved?

It didn't take long to find the names of the four men eventually arrested: *Pierce, Burgess, Fowler, and Agar*. Ginger's pulse leaped. The same surnames as the current victim and suspects. This couldn't be a coincidence. George Pierce and James Burgess Jr. were in custody. Simon Fowler, also known as Oscar Wright, was dead. Agar Jr. was nursing a bump on his head. Only Simon Fowler would've been old enough to have been part of the original robbery team.

Ginger read the piece again.

The elder Messrs Pierce and Fowler served time in England, only a few short years, and were released. Mr. Burgess Sr. had the misfortune of getting beaten up and subsequently fell ill. He was released but died not long afterwards. Agar however, ended up taking the blame for the robbery and was sent to Australia leaving behind a girlfriend and an illegitimate daughter.

Kay Agar.

Ginger quickly did the maths. Kay would be sixty-nine. Old enough to be Mrs. Simms.

CHAPTER TWENTY-NINE

Amongst motorcar horns and shouting pedestrians, Ginger sped back to the Crown Court. A sense of urgency to find Basil and for them to look for Mr. Agar pushed at her, but if there was something Ginger had learned during her time working as a private investigator, it was this: Criminals got nervous and unpredictable when one got close to the truth. And Ginger believed that a confrontation with Agar would not only get them one step closer to the truth but to danger as well.

Ginger parked in front of the Crown Court which was located on the same site as the police station and the prisons. The inquest was to take place in one of the meeting rooms. The inquest should be over soon . . . if it weren't already.

"I'm here for Chief Inspector Reed," Ginger announced to the clerk at the desk.

"I'm sorry, Mrs. Reed," the clerk responded. "Chief Inspector Reed has already left."

Oh mercy! They hadn't passed each other on the road, had they? "Did he perhaps leave a message? Say where he was going?"

The clerk rifled through a notepad. Ginger tapped the toe of her shoe impatiently. Time was of the essence. She could've knitted a hat by the time he'd finished flicking through his notes.

"Yes, he did," the clerk finally said. "He said if he missed you, he'd wait for you in the hotel restaurant."

GINGER DID a quick glance at their usual table but another couple, deep in conversation, occupied it. She scanned the room, first the window tables where she'd expect Basil to be seated then the tables in the centre of the room, and finally the stools along the bar. She recognised no one. Basil wasn't there.

Where is he?

"Hello, have you seen my husband?" Ginger asked a passing waiter. "Tall, hazel eyes, dark hair greying a little at the temples?"

He shook his head then nodded towards the back. "Check with Mr. Styles at the bar."

Mr. Styles, an older fellow with thick hair oiled back and friendly eyes, smiled when Ginger approached with the same question. "I only remember him because I remember you," he said with a wink. "He hasn't been here. Not today."

"Are you sure? When did you start your shift?"

"Madam, I own the place. My shift lasts from morning to night."

"Perhaps someone else served him?"

Mr. Styles stared beyond Ginger around the near empty room.

"There's only the two of us on at the moment." His eyes darted to the waiter Ginger had stopped a few minutes before. "I haven't seen him."

Ginger hurried past the hotel desk clerk and up the stairs to their room.

"Basil!" A quick scan of the room confirmed that her husband wasn't there and the dread building in her chest grew heavier. She let out a defeated breath. *Where is he?*

Her Boston terrier sat up on his haunches and, as if sensing his mistress' distress, let out a soft whimper. "Oh, Bossy," Ginger said. "Perhaps something came to light at the inquest. Perhaps he came to the same conclusion about Agar as I have."

If that were the case, then Basil had purposefully left her a misleading message at the Crown Court. The only reason he'd do something like that—and risk incurring her wrath—was if he were trying to protect her. Which meant he knew he was heading into danger.

Ginger's luggage was stacked in one corner of the room. The maid that Basil had arranged to help her unpack had hung her dresses in the wardrobe and sorted her shoes and hats. Ginger had kept one case to herself, a box the size of a large cigar case. She opened the bottom drawer of the bedside table, removed the case, and placed it on the silk quilt on the bed.

As she lifted the lid, she said a prayer of thanks for her first husband, Lord Daniel Gold. In the box lay a silver, palm-sized Remington Derringer—a gift from Daniel the evening before he left for war.

Ginger removed the pistol and slipped it into her handbag. She'd learned to trust her intuition over the years. Basil was in trouble.

"We're going for a motorcar ride, Boss," she said. Boss jumped off the bed and panted with anticipation. "But you have to promise to be a good boy and listen carefully to everything I say."

Boss' little tail wagged, and he looked up at Ginger with round brown eyes, as if to say, "You can count on me!"

Once in the motorcar, Ginger pressed the starter button, changed gears, and turned the machine towards Doncaster.

CHAPTER THIRTY

An earlier rainfall made the road to Doncaster mucky with muddy water-filled potholes. Ginger's urge to speed was thwarted. She didn't know what had happened to Basil, but her intuition was going off like a red alarm. *He's in trouble.* The words spun in her head.

Boss, getting tossed about by the dips and jerks, let out a low howl.

"I'm sorry, Bossy, but it can't be helped." Ginger hoped a tyre didn't blow or an axle give way. *A breakdown would be a disaster.* Ginger forced herself to go slower.

Finally, lights from the town appeared on the horizon. The police station lay in the direction of the Agar cottage. As anxious as she was to ease her mind that

Basil was okay, she knew it was prudent to make a quick stop.

The officer behind the counter was the same one who had been on duty the last time she and Basil were there. His eyes widened in recognition.

"Good evening, Mrs. Reed."

"Has my husband called in recently?"

The officer shook his head. "Not to my knowledge." He shouted over his shoulder towards the two adjoining rooms with doors wide open. "Has Chief Inspector Reed been in today?"

Both responses bellowed back were negative.

"Is there something I can help you with?"

"I'm heading out to the Agar place. Perhaps you could assign an officer to follow me out there."

"Why? Is there a problem?"

"I'm not sure. But if there is, I'll need help."

Doncaster civil servants hadn't yet budgeted for streetlights, gas or electric, outside the town centre, and Ginger had to depend on the headlamps of the motorcar and her own recollection of how to get to the Agar cottage.

She'd been trained during the war to note every detail—a habit, thankfully, that was still ingrained. Even though she'd only been to the cottage once, she remembered the landmarks along the way. A barren beech tree. An abandoned cart loaded with the remnants of bleached-out hay.

Ginger turned off the headlamps before turning down the lane. She didn't want Mr. Agar to know of her arrival. Strapping her handbag over her shoulder, she removed the Remington and a battery-operated torch.

She spoke carefully to her dog. "We're looking for Basil, Bossy. You need to be very quiet unless you find him." Basil had left a scarf in the motorcar, and Ginger held it up to Boss' nose. She placed a finger to her lips, the sign for quiet she'd taught Boss when he was a puppy, and then edged the motorcar door open.

The cottage was dark. *Agar was in bed? Postmen have early morning shifts; Agar would be accustomed to early nights. Or maybe, he's just not home.*

Is he inside watching me? Oh, mercy!

Ginger knocked on the door.

No answer.

She tried the door handle. It was unlocked and clicked open.

"Mr. Agar?"

She raced the torch beam around the room, which cast eerie shadows on the walls. The wooden floorboards creaked as she crossed the room.

"Basil?"

Boss sniffed around the room and whined.

"He's been here, hasn't he?" Ginger said.

Boss let out a single soft bark.

Mr. Agar didn't have electric lights. Ginger, now with nerves as tense as new telephone wires, had the small torch clamped between her teeth, and her arms stretched out, hands gripping the revolver. Her heart thumped in her chest. She had a gun, but he could be hiding anywhere.

"Bossy? We're alone, aren't we?"

Boss sniffed the wooden floor, whined and kept sniffing.

The living room and kitchen were empty, but that left the bedroom. A person could hide behind the door, under the bed, or in a wardrobe.

Ginger pushed the door open and pivoted quickly to check behind the door. The moment made her stumble—Mr. Agar preferred leaving his laundry on the floor it seemed—and the torch slipped from her mouth and rolled under the bed.

Complete darkness.

Beads of sweat formed on her brow and she bent low and reached under the bed. She grimaced at the thought of what she might touch under there, but most of all she was worried about Basil. She was wasting time!

Her fingers found the torch and she quickly got to

her feet, taking a second to brush the dust off her Molyneux frock.

To be thorough she flipped open the wardrobe doors, pistol cocked and ready, but found nothing that one wouldn't expect.

The house was empty.

That left the garden shed she'd noted at the back of the property.

The tightness in Ginger's chest grew painful, and she practically flew out of the rear door. *Where was that backup officer?*

Her heels caught in the damp soil, slowing her progress. Thankfully, her shoes were pumps, and she easily stepped out of them. The cold earth was a shock to her feet, but she didn't have time to entertain the discomfort. Her only thought was to reach the shed.

The garden shed was built of the same brick and stone as the cottage, with a weather-worn thatched roof. As Ginger drew closer, she glimpsed a sliver of light coming from under the wooden door that was shrunken slightly off its frame. A rusted padlock hung open. Someone was in there.

Boss started barking wildly.

Basil!

Ginger burst through the door, and the scene before her made her heart stop.

CHAPTER THIRTY-ONE

Basil lay on a wooden table. Blood ran down his face from a gaping wound on his head. His head lolled to one side. Ginger stared at his chest, willing it to move. It did. Basil was alive but unconscious.

Axe in hand, Mr. Agar stood near Basil's head.

"Mrs. Reed," he said looking amused. "This is a surprise. You're just in time for the main event." He pulled back on Basil's forehead, exposing his neck.

"No! Stop!" Ginger raised her pistol. "Step back and lower your weapon!"

Agar hesitated then did as commanded.

Boss started barking, his nose pointed towards the open door. Had the police found them? With her eye on Agar, she stepped to the side.

"It's okay, Boss. Come here."

The small dog grew silent and ran to his mistress.

It wasn't a policeman who entered the shed. An older lady was dressed in a common day frock that hung from her bosom to her ankles, rubber boots on her feet, and a shovel in her hand.

"Mrs. Griffiths?" Ginger said, unable to conceal her surprise. And yet, somehow Ginger wasn't surprised at all. The pieces started falling together.

"Hello, Mrs. Reed," the woman said. The oil lighting threw ominous shadows onto the walls, and Mrs. Griffiths' face took on the appearance of a ghoul. A smell of nervous sweat emanated from her.

Ginger caught sight of a red sticky substance on the edge of the shovel. Mud and blood. Her heart sank. "Did you kill the police officer?" That would explain why no one from the police station had shown up.

"That witless fellow who professes to keep the law around here? No, I don't think he's dead. He'll have a heck of a headache when he comes to, I'd wager."

"What are you doing here?" Ginger asked again. Her eyes darted to Basil, her gaze landing briefly on his chest until she saw it rise, and then back to the woman before her. She took a small step back, careful to be out of the shovel's reach.

Mrs. Griffiths didn't seem at all upset or shocked by the gruesome scene set before them.

"I live next door. I heard your dog bark. My son doesn't have a dog."

Ginger's gun had remained trained on Agar. "Of course. Your son. You're the elder Edward Agar's daughter."

"Yes, I am. I think it's time we were properly introduced. I'm Kay Agar. Like my mother before me, I've lived a life of ill repute. This is my illegitimate son."

"*You* got your son to kill Oscar Wright?" Ginger shook her head. "Or rather, Simon Fowler."

KayAgar chuckled. "See Edward? Why couldn't you be as clever as this one?"

Edward Agar slumped, and Ginger was relieved to see the axe hanging loosely in his hand, the head dragging on the wooden slats of the floor. Ginger let her pistol relax in kind.

"Why?" Ginger pressed. "Revenge?"

"Justice!" Kay spat. "My father was sent to Australia—albeit on another charge—and I never saw him again. But he would've come back, you know, if they hadn't cast all the blame on him. He wasn't here to defend himself. Do you know what it's like to grow up without a father, Mrs. Reed?"

Ginger had been blessed with a marvellous father, but she'd missed out on a mother.

"I know what it's like to grow up without a parent," she said. Ginger had to keep an eye on both the mother and son, each at opposite ends of the room, whilst ensuring that Basil's chest kept rising. Her mind raced. How would she disarm the Agars so she could get Basil to the hospital? Meanwhile, Ginger knew she had to keep the lady talking as she devised a plan.

"You were angry about that."

"Of course, I was. But I worked hard." She pointed at her greying head with a gnarly finger. "I have brains. I pulled myself out of poverty. But I never forgot what should've been mine. My father's share of the gold."

"So, you killed Mr. Fowler?"

"Well, technically, my son killed him." Kay Agar's gaze landed on her son. "I simply provided the bump on Edward's head." She wiggled the shovel, her apparent weapon of choice. "To make him look innocent, you see, so they wouldn't suspect him of delivering the head aboard the Flying Scotsman." Edward's hand moved to the back of his head, as if the mention of his mother's attack evoked pain.

Ginger was astounded. Some women weren't meant to be mothers.

"Fowler was the only one still alive." Kay chortled. "You should've seen his face when he realised who I was."

"And the others? The offspring? Why set up the jewel theft?"

"It was a test of character. I offered them a chance

to commit another train robbery, smaller in scope, I'll admit, but I am an old lady. If they declined, I'd leave them in peace. If they accepted, it was proof they were no better than their fathers before them, and would suffer in their stead."

"That was why you got your son to plant Mr. Fowler's head on the train. So, Mr. Pierce and Mr. Burgess would get caught, first for robbery, then for murder."

"Like I said, I knew you were clever."

"How did Miss Dansby get caught up in it?"

"Her stupid fiancé brought her in. Not my fault. Silly girl. Anyway, they were all to hang for Fowler's murder—poetic justice you see. And it would've gone to plan if you and your nosy husband hadn't got involved."

"I'm certain Inspector Sullivan would've solved the case."

Mrs. Simms smiled maliciously. "I'm certain he wouldn't have."

"You were going to kill him too?"

"You've got killing on the mind, Mrs. Reed. One doesn't have to kill a person to get them out of the way. Unless it's troublemakers like you and the chief inspector."

Mrs. Simms nodded at her son. Agar lifted his axe.

Ginger immediately fell into posture—legs apart,

arms out straight, finger on the trigger. "Drop it, or I'll shoot!"

Agar lifted a thick shoulder, looking defeated. "You'll have to shoot me then."

The obedient son raised the axe. Kay lunged at Ginger. Boss jumped on Kay, pushing her back. Ginger pulled the trigger. The axe fell.

Finally, sirens blared in the distance.

CHAPTER THIRTY-TWO

"Basil!"

Kay Agar had fallen against her own shovel and lay on the floor of the garden shed, bleeding. Her moans confirmed she was alive and Boss stood guard with his tiny white teeth bared, ensuring she didn't get back to her feet.

Edward Agar was also on the ground bleeding, but he didn't emit any sounds to indicate whether he was alive or not.

Ginger registered these facts but her focus was entirely on Basil. There was blood, a lot of it. Edward hadn't hit Basil in the throat with his axe, but he hadn't entirely missed his mark either.

"Basil?" Ginger placed two fingers around Basil's wrist, and held her breath as she waited for a pulse.

There, it was *there.* Her relief was short-lived as she determined the source of the blood—a nasty gash along the forearm where the axe had hit a vein. Though she didn't have Haley's nursing skills, she had acquired some knowledge of first aid whilst assisting the nurses in triage during the war. Forced to improvise, she used Boss' leash to fashion a tourniquet, slowing the bleeding. There was nothing sanitised in the shed and the best Ginger could do was to reach under her skirt and remove her slip which she used as a make-shift bandage.

She stroked Basil's face. "You're going to be fine, love. I'm here."

His eyes fluttered open as if it took all the energy he had in the world to do it. His lips separated, but Ginger placed her finger against them. "Don't talk now. Save your strength."

"Mrs. Reed?"

Ginger turned to the sound of Inspector Sullivan's voice.

"Inspector, we need an ambulance!"

"I got Chapman running to make the call." His gaze landed on Basil. "How is he?"

"I'm not a doctor, but I believe he'll be fine." Ginger squeezed Basil's hand as she said it. *Please be fine.*

As the inspector's eyes took in the room, Ginger could see him make a quick assessment: a lady who looked like their suspect Mrs. Griffiths, and the Doncaster postman, both disarmed and disabled. He narrowed his gaze at Ginger. "Do you mind telling me what happened?"

"With the Great Gold Robbery repeatedly coming up in our investigations, I felt I should do a bit of research on the topic. The surnames of all our suspects were in the reports: Pierce, Burgess, Fowler, and Agar. I put two and two together. Mr. Agar wasn't the victim of the crime, but the villain. I assumed he was the mastermind and a very fine actor, but I was wrong there." Ginger nodded towards the elderly lady on the ground. "That's Kay Agar, Edward Agar's mother."

"It's not Mrs. Griffiths?"

"No, that was an alias. She's the daughter of Edward Agar Senior, the man who took the blame for the Great Gold Robbery. She's the one who planned the murder and the robbery."

Inspector Sullivan whistled. "Both? To what end?"

"She was entrapping the descendants of her father's enemies. She wanted to see them hang for Fowler's murder. The robbery was the catalyst to stop the Flying Scotsman so that they would be implicated.

"But when I looked for Basil to tell him what I'd discovered, he was nowhere to be found. He must've put two and two together as well." Ginger imagined that Basil had indeed gone to the hotel to wait for her, but then decided to take a taxicab to Agar's cottage to test out his theory for himself. Ginger felt it was quite possible that he'd left without her as a protective gesture, to keep her out of harm's way. She'd lecture him about that another time.

"I came out here expecting to find him," she said softly, "but not like this."

Ginger turned as the first tear escaped. She didn't want Inspector Sullivan to witness her emotions. Had Edward's axe found its mark . . . It was too horrible to think about.

Inspector Sullivan squatted beside Edward Agar's body and checked for a pulse. "The bloke's alive."

"Good."

"Shot."

Ginger nodded.

"By you?"

"My pistol is registered." Basil had insisted she finally got it done.

Inspector Sullivan grunted. "All the same, I'll be bagging it for evidence."

Kay Agar began to stir. "It was all my idea," she muttered. "Edward was just a pawn."

"Did he kill Mr. Fowler?" the inspector asked. "Alias Mr. Wright?"

"My Edward lifted the axe and let it drop, but it was I who first plunged the knife in his back. At best he's an accessory. He won't hang for that."

"But you will," Ginger said.

Kay chortled. "Not if I die first."

CHAPTER THIRTY-THREE

Ginger knew how to shoot to kill. She also knew how not to, which was why Mr. Edward Agar was still alive. As soon as he was well enough to leave the hospital, he'd join his mother in prison awaiting trial for attempted robbery, murder, and attempted murder.

Basil had recovered from the nasty bump on his head but still complained about an occasional headache. However, the gash on his arm would leave a nasty scar.

When Basil had come to the cottage, Mr. Agar sneaked up behind him and hit him on the head with a shovel. Stronger than he looked, Mr. Agar had dragged Basil to the garden shed and tied him to the bench.

A week after his ordeal, Basil was now well enough to join Ginger for breakfast in the morning room in

Hartigan House. She smiled brightly at him when he entered.

"Good morning, love," she said. He took the seat beside her then leaned in for a kiss.

"Have I missed everyone else?"

"Ambrosia has come and gone, and Felicia has yet to arrive. She'd sleep past noon if I'd allow it."

"How do you prevent it?" Basil said after taking his first sip of breakfast coffee, a new habit since moving in. With that bump on his head, he probably needed something stronger to rouse him in the mornings. He continued, "She's an adult, after all."

"Yet, still being supported by me," Ginger returned. "I'm going to convince her to work at Feathers & Flair. It would be good for her to take on some responsibility. I might even join forces with Ambrosia and begin a search for a husband for Felicia in earnest!"

Basil chuckled. "Jolly good. It might actually keep you out of trouble."

Ginger tilted her head. "And what's going to keep you out of trouble, my dear?"

"Touché, love, touché."

Mrs. Beasley joined Lizzie as they rolled in the breakfast offerings: bacon and eggs, fried kippers, and hot rolls.

"Smells heavenly," Ginger said.

"Thank you, madam." Mrs. Beasley, a fleshy lady—almost as wide as she was tall—looked to Basil. Ginger noticed how her staff continued to act stiffly and awkwardly around her new husband, and she wished there was something she could do to put them at ease.

Basil smiled at the cook. "I've never eaten so well."

Mrs. Beasley let out an excited breath. "It's my pleasure to serve you, sir."

She bustled back to the kitchen leaving Lizzie, the younger, slimmer maid, to finish serving.

"Would you like more tea, sir? Madam?"

"We're drinking coffee at the moment," Ginger replied.

Lizzie bobbed. "I'm sorry, I should've noticed."

"It's quite all right, Lizzie," Ginger said kindly. "Miss Gold is sure to want tea and should be down soon."

Pippins shuffled into the morning room. "Madam, your morning papers have arrived."

Ginger subscribed to several newspapers, including the *Boston Globe* and *New York Times*. They were always a week late, being shipped over the Atlantic, but Ginger didn't mind. She liked to keep up with the latest in politics and the social scene. Occasionally, she came across names she recognised, including her socially reckless half-sister Louisa, whose young, pretty face often showed up in the society pages. If anything drastic happened in America, the London papers and BBC radio would report it.

She unfolded the *London Morning Press.* Mrs. Griffiths, alias Mrs. Simms, alias Kay Agar, had been in the headlines for the last week, but today, her story had fallen below the fold. The mystery of how "Mrs. Simms" had "disappeared" from the Flying Scotsman had been explained. "Mrs. Griffiths" had had her disguise in her holdall. She'd simply changed out of her costume in the lavatory whilst Ginger, Basil, and Felicia were in the dining car. Being in the compartment at the back of the carriage had prevented the other passengers from noticing. The cane she had dispatched through window had come back with a partial print belonging to Kay Agar.

Lady Pennington was performing in London once again at the weekend. Hopefully this time she'd leave her jewels at home and no one would be tempted to follow her around for nefarious reasons. Ginger wondered about the Fishers, if they'd ever made it to Edinburgh. Basil was able to confirm that the couple were, in fact, married and not siblings. Mr. Doring had taken sick leave, and Ginger hoped his nerves would recover. Poor man. The businessmen, Mr. Whitley and Mr. Murray, were mentioned in the business section. It was happy news on their business venture. All had not been lost by their delay after all.

"Do you think Kay Agar will be hanged?" Ginger asked Basil as she patted butter on a roll. "At her age? In her condition?" They had learned that the old lady had been recently diagnosed with terminal cancer.

"I doubt it," Basil said as he dabbed his lips with a linen napkin. "Though perhaps she'd prefer a quick death."

Mr. Edward Agar had yet to go on trial, but his guilt was obvious, and with Basil's personal testimony, a jury would agree.

"I'm eternally thankful that you found me," Basil said. It wasn't the first time he'd expressed his gratitude, despite the fact he disliked Ginger carrying a pistol—something he'd made clear to her on more than one occasion. Ginger wasn't sure if that was because she might at some time be in a situation where she'd need one—and obviously she had—or if it was because the Remington had been a gift to her from her late husband, Lord Daniel Gold.

"I'm happy to have saved your life, darling," she replied lightly. "In fact, I believe I've done it more than once."

"Can I not say the same?"

"I suppose you can."

"We're two peas in a pod, aren't we?" Basil said with a glint in his hazel eyes.

Ginger agreed. "Two peas who've yet to go on their honeymoon!"

"We must rectify that immediately," Basil said, "though, do you think we can leave Scotland for another time?"

"Most definitely," Ginger said. She had no desire to board another train. "We must fly somewhere. You can charter small planes now. We could go to France, Italy, even Greece."

"The thought of flying through the air in a tin can doesn't frighten you?"

Ginger shrugged. "It would be exciting. Think of the adventure!"

The rhythmic tapping of The Dowager Lady Gold's silver-handled walking stick could be heard down the passageway and was soon followed by the presence of the formidable lady. Upright in the manner that only a corset could achieve in one of advanced age, she wore a grey wool dress that draped over an ample bosom and ended at her ankles revealing short-top leather boots. Her grey hair was styled in a more fashionable shorter cut, incongruous with the rest of her attire.

"I heard voices and thought I'd come to sit. I've already had breakfast as I arise at a reasonable hour." Her eyes flashed at Ginger with a slight look of disapproval. "But I wouldn't mind another cup of tea."

Felicia stumbled in with a yawn, just barely covering her opened mouth with her hand before the yawn took over her face.

"Good heavens, child!" Ambrosia said. "I keep telling you that you get to sleep too late in the evening. Why must you gallivant about the town every night?"

Felicia slid into a chair and poured a cup of coffee. "I don't gallivant about every night, Grandmama. Life's been so stressful these last few days, I had to have some fun to balance it out."

"Why is it stressful for you?" Ambrosia said. "You're not the one getting arrested." She narrowed her eyes at her charge. "*Are you?*"

"Not this time, Grandmama."

Ginger didn't often side with her former grandmother-in-law, but when it came to the somewhat reckless flapper-girl lifestyle Felicia had adopted, she couldn't help but worry.

"I do hope you're being careful," Ginger said.

"Whatever do you mean?" Felicia said with a sly smile.

"I think you know what I mean."

Through the French windows, Ginger spotted Scout and Boss playing on the lawn; Scout tossed a short stick and Boss eagerly ran to retrieve it.

Ginger pushed away from the table. "Excuse me a moment whilst I say good morning."

Outside, she laughed at her charges. "My two favourite boys!"

Boss' little black-and-white head snapped up at the sound of her voice and sprinted like a miniature race-horse towards her. Ginger bent a knee to reach him and lifted him off the ground.

"Good morning, Bossy!"

Scout watched her shyly. He stuffed his fists into his trouser pockets and scuffed the grass with the toe of his shoe. His newsboy hat sat crookedly on short wheat-coloured hair.

"Good morning, Scout," Ginger said.

"G'morning, missus."

Ginger inclined her head, holding on to young Scout's gaze. Though eleven years old, he appeared younger. Growing up on the streets without proper food and care could do that to a lad. "Are you not happy to see me?"

"Of course, I am, missus. Uh, where's Mr. Reed?"

Ginger placed Boss on the ground as she answered. "He's eating breakfast." She knew Scout was wary of another man moving into Hartigan House. Actually, not just another man, but another man in Ginger's life. "I thought you and I could spend a bit of time together this morning. Let's go and say hello to Goldmine, shall we?"

Scout's freckly face broke into a smile, his new adult teeth showing prominently. "All right, missus."

Ginger reached for Scout's small hand and said nothing about the dirt under his nails or how rough his palm was for one so young. He worked hard for his keep, helping Mrs. Beasley sweep the kitchen and Mr. Clement with the gardening and stable care, especially with Goldmine, Ginger's Akhal-Teke gelding. Scout never complained. He was young, but old enough to remember how hard life was alone on the mean streets of London.

Scout was her ward, not her son. As a Lady, a baron's wife at that, adopting a street urchin would've been unthinkable. But now, as a police officer's wife?

That deep longing in her soul pinged again. She'd missed out on having children. Not a choice she'd made for herself, but one dished out to her. Over time she accepted her lot and found fulfillment in her work and her charities.

Goldmine whinnied a greeting when Ginger entered the stable with Scout. She'd like to have thought the gelding was happy to see her, but it was apparent that the horse's affection lay with Scout. The lad crawled through the fence of Goldmine's stall and wrapped his thin arms around its muscular neck. Goldmine's golden coat shone like silk, due in part to his exotic breed and in part to Scout's dedication to regular grooming.

Ginger picked up an apple from the bin and flattened her palm as she reached for Goldmine over the fence. "Hey, boy," she said softly. Goldmine tickled her hand with his soft nose before taking a bite of the apple.

"That's his second treat today," Scout said. "I've given 'im one too."

"Some days are two-treat days," Ginger said. When the apple had disappeared, she rubbed Goldmine's head. "You both did such a great job at the wedding."

"And Boss too," Scout corrected.

"Oh yes, and Boss too." Ginger smiled at her charge. "Scout, why don't you eat with me and Mr. Reed this morning?" She'd left mid-meal and would have to get Mrs. Beasley to reheat it anyway. Hopefully, Ambrosia would have become restless and left the morning room by now. Ginger didn't want to deal with her judgmental looks or worse, comments, yet.

"Really?" Scout shoved his fists into his trouser pockets again and studied the floor of the stable.

Ginger knelt to get to eye level with her ward. "What is it, Scout? Don't you like Mr. Reed?"

"He's a copper, missus. My kind don't mix well with his kind."

"I see. Well, how about we forget about his job?

You just think of him as my husband and a nice man who cares about you."

"Why would he care about me, missus? I'm nuffin' to 'im."

Ginger ignored the fact that Scout had reverted to dropping his *h's* recently. He'd been doing so well with his speech patterns until now.

"He cares about you because he cares about what I care about," Ginger explained. "And I care about you. Plus, I think he just genuinely likes you."

Scout's chin jutted up, his eyes wide and hopeful. "Really. You think so?"

"I do. Now—" Ginger retook his hand. "Let's go and have a wash."

BASIL WOULD'VE GONE crazy just lying around if it weren't for Ginger's company. Morris had told him to stay at home until he could walk in a straight line and properly use his gammy arm. Basil still wanted to take Ginger away somewhere so they could be *alone*, however, whiling the time away with his new wife had its own pleasures. The upper floor library housed an impressive number of books, and he and Ginger liked to snuggle in front of the fire to read together. Ginger did most of the reading because the knot on his head caused headaches that worsened when he tried to read.

They were lounging on the settee in the sitting room; Ginger's back was pressed up against his chest, her legs stretched out, and a pair of her many shoes toppled on the Persian carpet beneath them. Ginger had got Pippins to light the gas lanterns, freshly stoke the fire in the stone fireplace, and put American jazz on the gramophone. The mood was cosy and romantic. Best of all, they were alone, though when Felicia had stepped in, it had taken a sharp look for her to turn on her heel. Nonetheless, she squawked about it the entire way to the drawing room.

Ginger laid the book down on her lap. "Haley and I used to meet together for a glass of brandy at the end of the day," Ginger said. "This was her favourite spot. I sat over there."

Basil's gaze followed hers to a plush wingback chair.

"Definitely not enough room for both of us in that," he said.

"Some traditions are worth changing."

Boss' pointy ears jutted up from his satin bed by the fireplace. He stretched short, bony legs, stubby tail pushed up, before trotting over to Ginger and jumping on her lap.

Basil nuzzled his nose into her neck. "I suppose I might as well just get use to sharing you with a smelly mongrel."

Boss whined.

"He's not smelly, and he's not a mongrel!" Ginger laughed. She sniffed Boss' head. "Okay, perhaps a little smelly. Boss, you need a bath!"

Boss whined again, distinctly not in favour of this declaration.

They were interrupted by a knock on the door and the balding head of Ginger's butler—Basil's butler now—poked in.

"Sorry to disturb you, madam, but the afternoon post has arrived, and there's a letter from America. I thought you'd want to see it."

Ginger pushed off the settee, nearly breaking into a run. She stretched out her arm. "Oh yes, Pips! Let me see it!"

Pippins extended the silver platter, and Ginger picked up the top letter. "Thank you, Pips. I'll read the others later."

"You're welcome, madam." Pippins cornflower-blue eyes twinkled with affection. Basil knew the story. Clive Pippins was a lifer, having served the Hartigan family since Ginger was a child. Their relationship went beyond mistress and servant. Ginger's green eyes smiled warmly as she watched the septuagenarian leave.

"You're not having an affair with your butler, are

you?" Basil asked with a grin. "I mean, I can see the appeal, and you obviously are a catch."

Ginger returned to the settee and slapped his leg playfully. "You're the only man for me, Mr. Reed."

"So?" Basil said, nodding to the envelope in Ginger's hand.

"It's from Boston. At first, I thought it was from Haley, but it's from my stepmother's housekeeper, Molly McPhail. She was my maid from when I arrived in Boston with my father at eight years of age. She's one of the best people I know."

Basil read the concern in her eyes. "I'm sure if there were something amiss with your family, you would've received a telegram from them, and not a letter from the housekeeper."

Ginger carefully opened the envelope with the help of a long fingernail. She read:

Dearest Mrs. Reed,

Please forgive this late letter of congratulations on your recent marriage. I'm afraid I only learned of your nuptials recently. As happenstance would have it, I've become reacquainted with a friend of yours, a Dr. Haley Higgins, and she relayed the happy news.

. . .

GINGER'S HEAD BOBBED UP. "I wonder why she hadn't heard. Surely, Louisa and Sally spoke of it?"

Basil knew the question wasn't for him. He remained silent, and Ginger continued to read.

PERHAPS YOU'VE NOT BEEN INFORMED, but my position with Mrs. Hartigan has recently been terminated. She found me at fault for Miss Hartigan's latest escapade, her running off to London.

"SALLY!" Ginger protested. "My stepmother can be so unfair! I would've brought Molly with me to London, but she was too frightened to travel such a long distance across the ocean."

"HOWEVER, I'm writing to you with good news. Dr. Higgins has brought me into her employ, and, please forgive me for saying so, she's so much nicer than Mrs. Hartigan and far easier to please. If you haven't heard from Dr. Higgins recently, it's because she's terribly busy with her new job at the morgue. All the crime in Boston these days. Prohibition has backfired terribly in

my opinion. I never read about so many deaths and murders in the city as I have of late. Dr. Higgins is quite heavy-hearted about the death of her brother, and I hope to add a little lightness to the home. You can't live in sorrow all the time, I tell her.

Oh, Dr. Higgins just came home. She's requested a postscript. I'm sure you won't mind.

SINCERELY,

Molly

PS: Dear Ginger, I suppose you'll be reading this after you've returned from your honeymoon. I hope it went well and that you and that dashing new husband of yours stayed out of trouble. Somehow, I doubt it!

Basil laughed. "She knows you well."

Ginger pressed the letter to her chest. "Haley and Molly! My two favourite Americans in all the world."

Basil leaned over to kiss his wife but was stopped by the aggravated barking of the dog.

"Bossy, it's okay," Ginger said as she patted the animal's head. "It's only Basil."

"And I thought I'd have to be jealous over your butler, but now I fear it might be your dog."

Ginger moved Boss to her other side, then grabbed Basil by the tie.

"I hope you mean to lead me to the bedroom, Mrs. Reed."

"How scandalous! It's only the afternoon."

He nuzzled her neck. "I'm sure it's evening somewhere in the world."

The End.

Read on for news from La Plume Press.

NOTE FROM THE AUTHOR

THE GREAT GOLD ROBBERY

This is where I confess to taking massive liberties with the real life Great Gold Robbery, also know as the Great Train Robbery of 1855. In my defence, there are others who have done so before me and probably most notably is the 1978 Sean Connery film *The Great Train Robbery*.

If you're a history buff, you'll recognize my use of some names and details associated with the robbery. I consider that a nod to the real event. In no way have I tried to, or desired to, pass off the version of history found in this fictional story as fact.

MORE FROM LA PLUME PRESS

I hope you enjoyed *Murder Aboard the Flying Scotsman.*

**** I've started a new series featuring Ginger's good friend, Haley Higgins, but rest assured, there will be more Ginger Gold to come. Read on for news about book 9 -** ***Murder at the Boat Race*****.**

But first, let me introduce you to the **Higgins & Hawke Mysteries**. If you're a fan of Rizzoli & Isles, you love this series. Set in Boston in the 1930s, it features two strong yet very different women.

Haley Higgins, whom you already know, is a intelligent, steady-as-she-goes, assistant pathologist. Determined to solve the crime *du jour,* she hasn't forgotten about her brother's murder, a case that has been cold for seven years.

Samantha Hawke is a hard-working and hard-edge investigative journalist trying to make it in a man's world. She has a daughter and mother-in-law to support and not quite enough money to do it.

An unlikely team, Higgins & Hawke find themselves working together to solve crimes during the depression era.

GET IT NOW

Death by Rum Running. . .

It's the hot and humid East Coast summer of 1931 and seven years since Dr. Haley Higgins' brother Joe was murdered. The case is cold. The Boston Police Department may have given up on finding Joe Higgins' killer, but Haley never will. She's serious and savvy and has what it takes to hold up under depressive times. At least she finds some satisfaction doing her part as the city pathologist's assistant in solving other crimes.

Investigative reporter Samantha Hawke ~ byline Sam Hawke ~ is blond, beautiful and broke, no thanks to her no good husband who's been on the lam for over six years. Her position at the Boston Daily Record is more than a job ~ it's payback.

When a man is found dead at the Bell in Hand Tavern on Union Street, Haley and Samantha are both working the case. Haley's looking for justice and Samantha's after recognition and a raise. They may want the same thing ~ to catch a killer ~ but it turns out they may need each other to solve this case before becoming the next victims.

AMAZON

GINGER GOLD MYSTERIES BOOK 9!

MURDER AT THE BOAT CLUB

Murder's a Stroke of Bad Luck!

The 77th Boat Races between Oxford and Cambridge Universities is an popular annual event, and Mrs. Ginger Reed is excited to attend for the first time, especially since the son of a good friend of her new husband, Chief Inspector Basil Reed, is racing for Oxford.

When tragedy strikes, and a very unusual murder presents itself, *Lady Gold's Investigations* is hired to take on the case. Can Ginger break the case before another young man is murdered?

Read on AMAZON
or order from your favorite books store.

Introducing LADY GOLD INVESTIGATES!

Ginger Gold has opened her own private investigation office!

This short story companion series to Ginger Gold Mysteries has the clever Mrs. Ginger Reed, aka Lady Gold, and her adventurous sister-in-law Felicia taking on clients who've got all sorts of troubles. This first volume consists of *The Case of the Boy who Vanished* and *The Case of the Missing Fox Stole.*

A companion series to Ginger Gold Mysteries, each volume is approximately 20 thousand words or 90 pages. A bite size read perfect for a transit commute home, time spent waiting at an appointment, or to settle into sleep at night. Get your coffee, tea or glass of wine and snuggle in!

Read on AMAZON
or order from your favorite books store.

GINGER GOLD'S JOURNAL

Sign up for Lee's readers list and gain access to **Ginger Gold's private Journal.** Find out about Ginger's Life before the SS *Rosa* and how she became the woman she has. This is a fluid document that will cover her romance with her late husband Daniel, her time serving in the British secret service during World War One, and beyond. Includes a recipe for Dark Dutch Chocolate Cake!

It begins: **July 31, 1912**

How fabulous that I found this Journal today, hidden in the bottom of my wardrobe. Good old Pippins, our English butler in London, gave it to me as a parting gift when Father whisked me away on our American adventure so he could marry Sally. Pips said it was for me to record my new adventures. I'm ashamed I never even penned one word before today. I think I was just too sad.

This old leather-bound journal takes me back to that emotional time. I had shed enough tears to fill the ocean and I remember telling

Father dramatically that I was certain to cause flooding to match God's. At eight years old I was well-trained in my biblical studies, though, in retro-spect, I would say that I had probably bordered on heresy with my little tantrum.

The first week of my "adventure" was spent with a tummy ache and a number of embarrassing sessions that involved a bucket and Father holding back my long hair so I wouldn't soil it with vomit.

I certainly felt that I was being punished for some reason. Hartigan House—though large and sometimes lonely—was my home and Pips was my good friend. He often helped me to pass the time with games of I Spy and Xs and Os.

"Very good, Little Miss," he'd say with a twinkle in his blue eyes when I won, which I did often. I suspect now that our good butler wasn't beyond letting me win even when unmerited.

Father had got it into his silly head that I needed a mother, but I think the truth was he wanted a wife. Sally, a woman half my father's age, turned out to be a sufficient wife in the end, but I could never claim her as a mother.

Well, Pips, I'm sure you'd be happy to know that things turned out all right here in America.

•

MORE FROM LEE STRAUSS

On AMAZON

GINGER GOLD MYSTERY SERIES (cozy 1920s historical)

Cozy. Charming. Filled with Bright Young Things. This Jazz Age murder mystery will entertain and delight you with its 1920s flair and pizzazz!

Murder on the SS Rosa

Murder at Hartigan House

Murder at Bray Manor

Murder at Feathers & Flair

Murder at the Mortuary

Murder at Kensington Gardens

Murder at St. George's Church

Murder Aboard the Flying Scotsman

Murder at the Boat Club

Murder on Eaton Square

Murder on Fleet Street

LADY GOLD INVESTIGATES (Ginger Gold companion short stories)

Volume 1

Volume 2

Volume 3

HIGGINS & HAWKE MYSTERY SERIES (cozy 1930s historical)

The 1930s meets Rizzoli & Isles in this friendship depression era cozy mystery series.

Death at the Tavern

Death on the Tower

Death on Hanover

A NURSERY RHYME MYSTERY SERIES (mystery/sci fi)

Marlow finds himself teamed up with intelligent and savvy Sage Farrell, a girl so far out of his league he feels blinded in her presence - literally - damned glasses! Together they work to find the identity of @gingerbreadman. Can they stop the killer before he strikes again?

Gingerbread Man

Life Is but a Dream

Hickory Dickory Dock

Twinkle Little Star

THE PERCEPTION TRILOGY (YA dystopian mystery)

Zoe Vanderveen is a GAP—a genetically altered person. She lives in the security of a walled city on prime water-front property along side other equally beautiful people with extended life spans. Her brother Liam is missing. Noah Brody, a boy on the outside, is the only one who can help ~ but can she trust him?

Perception

Volition

Contrition

LIGHT & LOVE (sweet romance)

Set in the dazzling charm of Europe, follow Katja, Gabriella, Eva, Anna and Belle as they find strength, hope and love.

Sing me a Love Song

Your Love is Sweet

In Light of Us

Lying in Starlight

PLAYING WITH MATCHES (WW2

history/romance)

A sobering but hopeful journey about how one young Germany boy copes with the war and propaganda. Based on true events.

A Piece of Blue String (companion short story)

THE CLOCKWISE COLLECTION (YA time travel romance)

Casey Donovan has issues: hair, height and uncontrollable trips to the 19th century! And now this ~ she's accidentally taken Nate Mackenzie, the cutest boy in the school, back in time. Awkward.

Clockwise

Clockwiser

Like Clockwork

Counter Clockwise

Clockwork Crazy

Clocked (companion novella)

Standalones

As Elle Lee Strauss

Seaweed

Love, Tink

ABOUT THE AUTHOR

Lee Strauss is a USA TODAY bestselling author of The Ginger Gold Mysteries series, The Higgins & Hawke Mystery series (cozy historical mysteries), A Nursery Rhyme Mystery series (mystery suspense), The Perception series (young adult dystopian), The Light & Love series (sweet romance), The Clockwise Collection (YA time travel romance), and young adult historical fiction with over a million books read. She has titles published in German, Spanish and Korean, and a growing audio library.

When Lee's not writing or reading she likes to cycle, hike, and play pickleball. She loves to drink caffè lattes and red wines in exotic places, and eat dark chocolate anywhere.

For more info on books by Lee Strauss and her social media links, visit leestraussbooks.com. To make sure you don't miss the next new release, be sure to sign up for her readers' list!

Did you know you can follow your favourite authors on Bookbub? If you subscribe to Bookbub — (and if you don't, why don't you? - They'll send you daily emails alerting you to sales and new releases on just the kind of books you like to read!) — follow me to make sure you don't miss the next Ginger Gold Mystery!

www.leestraussbooks.com
leestraussbooks@gmail.com